IN A COLD OPEN FIELD

By Sheila Solomon Klass

Fiction

In a Cold Open Field
A Perpetual Surprise
Bahadur Means Hero
Come Back on Monday

Fiction for Young Adults

A Shooting Star: A Novel about Annie Oakley
Next Stop: Nowhere
Rhino
Kool Ada
Credit-Card Carol
Page Four
The Bennington Stitch
Alive and Starting Over
To See My Mother Dance
Nobody Knows Me in Miami

Memoir

Everyone in this House Makes Babies

IN A COLD OPEN FIELD

A NOVEL BY

SHEILA SOLOMON KLASS

BLACK HERON PRESS
POST OFFICE BOX 95676
SEATTLE, WASHINGTON 98145

Published by:
>   Black Heron Press
>   Post Office Box 95676
>   Seattle, Washington 98145

For my mother and father
and brother

ONE

Sunday, May 13, 1951

"M is for the many things she gave me—"

The lean, broken-nosed sideshow barker in jeans and shiny, black plastic frontier-jacket moaned the song as he roamed back and forth in front of the freak museum. The blonde custard-stand girl stood transfixed, gaping at him, and this pleased him so he sang higher up in his nose.

"O is for—"

Passers-by stopped to listen blocking Momma's way.

She began to edge away from the crowded Boardwalk booths, picking her path carefully amid the unruly holiday throng.

She clicked little sounds of annoyance with her tongue, but no one seemed to notice.

No mature and mustached gentile gentleman bowed from the waist and moved out of her way.

No tall, clear-eyed lad gallantly took her arm

and led her through the crush, declaiming as he went:

> She's somebody's mother, boys, you know
> For all she's aged and poor and slow;
>
> And I hope some fellow will lend a hand
> To help my mother, you understand
>
> If ever she's poor and old and gray
> When her own dear boy is far away...

She had loved that poem ever since she'd learned it in the fifth grade. It had so much *feeling*.

But no one, young or old, now took the least notice of her.

And to think that once she had been young and pretty, and an accountant had courted her.

A Certified Public Accountant.

"Ladies and Gentlemen—"the barker shouted at the crowd—"The Pheenomenon of the 1951 Boardwalk: MADAME MYRA, The Bearded Lady!"

He half-turned to watch as his star came swiveling out onto the small exhibition block.

"See her genuwine beard. Note that real mustache. A marvel if I do say so myself." He shook his head at the wonder of it all. "Even though today is a holiday, folks, our admission price remains the same.

Fifty cents. Step right up."

Nobody moved.

"Come on—" he cajoled. "See our show. See Sammy the Sword-Swallower and Lu-Lou, half man and half woman. Right this way."

The crowd began to disperse just as Momma was making her way around the far side. As she passed close to the freak, she glanced up and then quickly averted her eyes.

Madame Myra was rosy-cheeked and round-faced, wrapped in a faded blue chenille housecoat. Her beard was thin and wispy, exactly like the beard of Rabbi Avrom Zoffar, that stern man who had lectured Momma about accepting God's will.

What did he know?

As if you could turn off the weeping of your heart's blood like a faucet.

Momma glanced up at Madame Myra one more time, and she shuddered at a resemblance that struck closer to home. For years, in secret, she had been plucking coarse ugly hairs; here was the horrible hairy phantom realized. She quickened her step.

There was something wrong with people who hung around a freak show on Mother's Day.

She moved away listening to the screams of the roller-coaster riders as their cars topped the rise and careened down the drop. All around her milled the population of the Boardwalk. Surely they all lived nearby. For as long as she could remember, they'd looked the same; the hot-dog-and-French-fry fanciers, mouths rimmed with catsup; the long-tongued custard lickers and popcorn-into-gaping-jaw tossers; the knees-akimbo bench sitters pleasuring themselves in cheap and vulgar ways.

Momma thought cotton candy an abomination.

She did not go on rides.

She had too few teeth for popcorn.

Hebrew National would never convince her that they didn't grind an occasional pig into their hot dogs.

So what was she, Momma, doing here now with sand in her sister Lily's black, ugly, hand-me-down oxfords? Never in her long New York life—she was born here, the daughter of immigrant Hungarian parents—never had she thought of Coney Island in any but a scornful way.

It was never more to her than a shoddy fraud, a spread of sand and a lot of noise, a bunch of shameless bums half naked on the hot gritty beach, and worse bums and their *bumikers* writhing and bending in the dirt beneath the Boardwalk, fleshworms wriggling about in the murky shade.

The few times she'd found it necessary to walk down there, Momma had kept her body stiff and straight, and she'd averted her eyes from the nasty activities.

Of one thing she was positive: None of the shameless ones were Jews!

She had a clear, hard, fixed code formed in her early years—she knew what was right and it never changed—it was the bedrock combination of the Ten Commandments and the Good Old Days.

Today was no exception. Today her husband, Sol, was praying in Williamsburg. He talked so much to God, he had little conversation left for her.

Today her son Ben was unaccounted for somewhere on the other side of the earth. In Korea, God alone knew where.

Today Coney Island was the same as usual, worse than usual, noisier, dirtier.

She did not stop to sit though her arthritic heel was stiff and fiery; each time she set her foot down, prongs of pain stabbed up into her ankle.

To sit was weakness. To sit was pleasure and she wanted no pleasure. Particularly on this warm Sunday afternoon in May that should have been hers by right, she wanted nothing of this world.

In the crowd around her young merrymakers bought red rose and pink carnation corsages labeled "MOM" in gilt on the bright ribbons; they won plush snakes and Kewpie dolls for Mother, took roller-coaster rides sitting next to her and exulted at her spirit, yelled and joked and pushed about, celebrating maternity with beer and Pepsi and colored orange water.

Hurriedly—yet with exaggerated care because she was frightened that someone might step on her bad foot—Momma cut through the holiday crowd, and, clinging tightly to a pipe railing she edged her way down the ramp.

BUY MOTHER AN EAR OF CORN: jagged red letters on a torn muslin strip. No matter where she looked, she couldn't escape.

That soldier entering the TUNNEL OF LOVE!

God in heaven, how he slouched, shoulders rounded and belly a little forward like Ben taking it easy.

Momma waited at the railing a long time until the cars rolled out after the ride.

No, of course not.

Ben was taller, finer looking. This boy's features were coarse.

Were there always so many tall boys in uniform around? So many?

She turned away from the TUNNEL OF LOVE. And there on the Midway, beset by the crowds and the fierce rocketing noises, she paused and she wept. People stared and they cut a wide swath around her.

TWO

For Momma the day had been bad from its very beginning.

What was it this time?

This time it was the intermittent rattle of the living room window right over her studio couch.

It wasn't a loud noise; still, it was a noise. It was a nuisance.

That lousy landlady.

Sure. In 1946 *her* son had returned from the war whole.

What did she care about anyone else?

Not that Momma begrudged the son. How could any decent person begrudge him?

Still—she did begrudge him. It was nothing personal just the accidental fact of his living.

Why he? Why the landlady's great healthy son, a man with sons of his own now, why he *yes*—

—and not her own Ben?

She focused her unhappiness on small creaking floor noises and mumbling sounds coming from the bedroom.

"Sol?"

Annoyed, he raised his voice to let her know yes it was Sol.

Who else was she expecting? Justice Frankfurter maybe was saying his morning prayers in her front room?

He chanted a line loudly then slipped back into his normal soft tones for the end of the morning service, the very last prayer.

He was a small gentle man whom life had so altered that of his sweet manliness all that was left was a quiet and apologetic timidity. This last prayer was very dear to him; he always recited it attentively.

"He is our God and there is no other. Our King is TRUTH and there is none besides Him: as it is written in His law, 'Know therefore this day and reflect in thine heart that the Lord He is God, in heaven above, and on earth beneath there is none else."

His prayers were softly spoken.

Sol did not respect those who bellowed their allegiance to God. He reasoned that since the Almighty was all-mighty, He could hear.

And, besides, Momma was such a light sleeper, if the morning prayers were louder than a whisper, she could also hear.

Recognizing the last prayer, Momma began to wonder aloud. "Where is he off to on a Sunday morning so early?"

This she asked of the shabby living room. "Always busy with nothing."

Now she addressed herself to the scarred drop-leaf table.

"Where did it get him?"

Her mouth was tainted with the aftertaste of sleep. She slid her tongue along the gums trying to wash away the unpleasantness.

If Dentyne could clean your teeth while it was in your mouth, why shouldn't your tongue?

Cats licked their kittens and it never hurt them. Once, in *Believe It or Not* by Ripley, long ago, she had read that a cow always licked its newborn calf clean, licked the whole afterbirth off. So, what harm?

Her tongue touched the empty sunken places along her gums where teeth had once been.

So few left. It was hard to believe.

Favoring her arthritic leg with its swollen heel—now covered by a clocked man's sock, its nightly protective sheath—she used her good leg to wind the sheet up off the side of the couch so it wouldn't drag on the floor.

She glanced over her head at the Big Ben on

the mantelpiece.

Seven. A rotten seven o'clock on a Sunday morning. When a person couldn't sleep, what did time matter?

Still, it did matter.

America was a democracy.

Why should the window always rattle even when there was no wind? Was it for this our boys gave their lives?

She shuddered and closed her eyes so she wouldn't have to see the cracked yellow walls, the water-stained ceiling, the bare bulb hanging on its wire and trailing a dusty gray pull-string.

It was best not to notice these things; in that way only could a person live.

Yawning, she sat up and adjusted her cotton slip so that she was completely covered.

Then, cautiously, she lowered her feet over the side.

She was a broad-boned heavy woman with a ravaged face.

Her short hair, once the color of coal, was yellow-gray and ragged. Her nose was straight and decent-sized, her cheekbones high and her sunken eyes an ordinary guileless brown. The lines of her nose and mouth were deep and cadaverous. Discontent had assisted age in sucking in the cheeks and mouth and lengthening the jaw.

Her pale skin was rough and porous; hands, face, and neck raw from too vigorous scrubbing and innocent of emollients. The fingers of both hands were striated and flaky, pie crust texture.

She slept in her slip so she had only to put on yesterday's clothes, a gray cotton skirt and a gray print blouse on which clumps of lavender flowers were barely discernible.

A quick trip to the toilet, a perfunctory washing-up and she was ready.

She went into the dismal kitchenette in which she had spent her life, pulled the light-cord—only in the late afternoon did a patch of sunlight penetrate this cell—then began making his breakfast.

Juice, poached eggs, slices of leftover challah, the Sabbath bread.

Back and forth she trudged from kitchenette to living room carrying food.

A single place was set on the table.

Afterward, she would eat as she had eaten during much of her married life.

Alone.

Sol came in. Thin, gray-haired, he had once been taller than she, but his body was bent forward now in the garment-worker's perpetual bow.

She was surprised to see him fully dressed, his indoor cap, the black yarmulke, already replaced by his fedora. "Where are you going in such a hurry?"

16

she asked as she carried in the poached eggs floating in water.

"Coffee. Pour it now so it will be cool when it's time to drink." He said that at every meal, but she never heeded him.

Hot seemed to her a virtue for coffee.

"Hurry, hurry, the whole life is hurry—" she observed, as she brought in a cup of milky coffee.

Dilute was another virtue.

She set the coffee down noisily. Without repeating the question directly, she was determined that he should answer it.

"I'm going to shul," he said, his mouth full of challah and egg. "Last week they didn't have a minyan on Sunday morning, so the rabbi asked me, 'Greenfield, you'll come on Sunday in the morning and help out?' I told him I am not so well and I must eat at regular times. 'Eat, then come,' he said. 'God will understand.' So then what could I say?"

"Not even a minyan," she marveled. "Not even ten men to hold a proper service in a shul like that with stained glass windows and plush seats even upstairs in the women's section, a shul where it was once so crowded on Yom Kippur a person couldn't get through the door. What times we live in."

She carried the egg plate back into the kitchenette.

"Maybe Rabbi Zoffar should call you *Mr. Greenfield,*" she suggested.

He never knew what she'd come up with these days. He blew on his coffee vigorously and began to take quick sips.

"Maybe if his manners were better his shul wouldn't be empty. Maybe he's not such a treasure of a rabbi."

"Because he couldn't work magic for you—for us—that's no reason to slander him. He can't change what happened. He's a rabbi not a miracle-worker. He told us truth; that was his duty. Even the Hasid, the Miracle-Worker, couldn't help us, so how could a plain *Misnagid* help? How?"

LIES, LIES, LIES!

The alarm shrilled in her brain.

Turning on both sink faucets all the way, she watched contentedly as the water gushed forth. Now she needn't hear him and she could gaze on clean water streaming forth.

God made everything possible. *He* could do anything.

The clogged drain kept the water in the sink. Too quickly it rose to the rim and she had to turn off the faucets.

Sol said nothing about the water. She did so many odd things these days, it was better to pretend not to notice.

"I'll be back later, Momma. Late in the afternoon."

"I won't be here. I'm going out. You know what day today is in America? Today is Mother's Day. My enemies should feel like I feel. So, today I am going away. Away!" Sobs choked her.

He squeezed his hands helplessly.

What could he do? He knew what day it was on the calendar, had thought of buying her a card or a geranium then decided not to mention it at all.

Some things should not be spoken but carried silently like stones in the heart.

Father's Day was coming too.

The calendar was full of days.

If only he could do something for her.

But if the rabbi with all his wisdom could do nothing, what could he—he who was only the husband—what could he possibly do?

THREE

Her blouse was drenched with tears. In her small money pouch was a handkerchief, a bit of white cloth already damp. Never mind. She could manage with it. It was cheaper than Kleenex.

She used it now to wipe her eyes and then the tip of her nose. She owned no large pocketbook, had never since she was married owned one. Just the tiny metal-clasped purse was enough for her. She reduced her needs to suit it.

While stuffing the handkerchief away, she glanced up. And there it was, summoning her from across the street.

GYPSY PRINCESS * ZOE *
ASTRALAGY READINGS
HEALER AND ADVISER
FREE CONSULTASHIONS

Her far-sighted eyes focused first on the letters and then on the whole storefront.

In one window there was an enormous inked diagram of a human head cut into sections by wormy, thick, black lines. In the other window was the paste-board sign that had attracted her.

She didn't stop right there in the middle of the street and cross over to the shop. She kept right on walking to the corner, to the safety zone, exhilarated by the storm of proof that pounded within her.

This then was why she was in Coney Island.

This then was why she had turned off the Boardwalk onto this particular street.

The BMT station was on Stillwell Avenue but had she ended up there? No. She had found her true destination.

. Here.

A giggle escaped Momma then another and still another, girlish noises to match her girlish excitement.

You, Momma, have a rendezvous with destiny.

Her mind rang with the dramatic promise made daily by the master-of-ceremonies of her favorite radio quiz program. He always introduced the jackpot question with that awesome promise.

And now it was Momma's turn and she was ready.

Leaning her arm on the lamppost, she rubbed her burning eyes against her wrist. Echoes of the old street game rang in her head.

Anyone around my base is it, ready or not,

here I come.

She prayed soundless, gratefully, giving thanks.

Blessed art Thou. Oh, Blessed. Blessed.

Impatient though she was, she waited. When the light turned green, she scurried across then turned to walk back along the block, slowly now, painfully, because the dash across the street had aggravated the pain in her heel.

Hop-limping along on the fortuneteller's side of the street, she passed rancid-smelling popcorn stands and a bald, weight-guesser whose obscene huge belly hung over the belt of his shorts like custard over a cone.

He embarrassed her by yelling, "Come right in, Madame. I'll guess your weight and whisper it into your ear. Correct weight within two pounds or you get a prize."

She was twenty pounds overweight but it was not his business. Or anyone else's. It was personal information.

She made up her mind increasing her resolve with every painful step.

I won't rush in.

That would be foolish.

Many fortunetellers are cheats.

Many only want the dollar in your hand.

Didn't one once take fifty cents from me and

claim that she could read the Lipton's teabag in my cup?

Who reads the tea leaves inside a bag?

What did she think I was, a fool?

I'm a New Yorker. I know my way around. I insisted that she read the leaves directly. I don't have so many fifty centses to give away.

Some fortunetellers are just good guessers. They really don't tell a person anything new.

What do I know about this Princess Zoe? Did I see her references? I don't know a thing, so I won't rush into her store.

"Easy, Momma. Don't get yourself into such an uproar," Ben used to say. I don't know where he picked up such funny expressions, but that's what he liked—likes—to say.

Because I am a woman, I know. This Princess will help me.

So strong is my intuition that it's pulling me, pulling me like a stretched elastic fastened to her door. She has a message for me, the spiritual message that I have been waiting for.

Not by chance did I find my way to Coney Island today, Sol, you can pooh pooh all you like, you and all the other kibitzers in the shul, and Rabbi Zoffar can sneeze and scoff with the rest of you, but there's more to this world than meets the eye. There are certain people with certain powers.

Never mind with Cabala.

A prophet's mind is her own private Cabala.

As I was led here, so I followed.

I just must not let myself by fooled. I must not throw away money on nothing. On teabags.

Absolutely not.

Princess Zoe will have to prove herself.

First, I will test her. Then—when I am sure—only then will I trust her.

While formulating this devious strategy within, Momma strove to maintain an appearance of calm disinterest without. Once she had crossed the street, she was committed, and though she could not say what would follow she felt that it was pre-ordained.

Her whole life had been merely a preliminary to now.

Now was her time. She would truly begin to live.

Exultantly she stepped forward—right into a pile of soft dog mess.

She had to stop a long time and scrape her filthied shoe on the curbstone.

Then along the broken pavements she scuffed, past stores and booths, sights and signs and souvenirs, head high and lips pursed speculatively. An out-of-town sight-seer, a tourist was her pose.

As she neared the storefront, her breathing

quickened to panting. Short, noisy breaths gusted from her throat.

It took tremendous effort to gain control: first inhale then exhale, then inhale and exhale. Her heart, at last, obeyed.

The window with the sign that had miraculously summoned her from across the street was irreproachably clean!

Glass Wax.

Her mind paid a housewife's tribute.

Newspapers and water never polished such a window no matter how hard a person rubbed. Science was marvelous.

The window was in itself a recommendation.

A crook wouldn't bother to wash windows with Glass Wax at forty-nine cents a can. A crook wouldn't take such care to rub the spots off in the corners.

Green plastic curtains with great red poinsettias stamped on them were tied back at either side framing the window like a Christmas scene.

Beneath the sign was a hand-lettered message:

IF THERE IS HELP ON EARTH IT CAN BE
FOUND THRU PRINCESS ZOE, SPIRITUAL
HEALER AND READER. NOT TO BE
CONFUSED WITH OTHER COMMON

ORDINARY IMPERSONATERS. SHE
ADVISES ON ALL AFFAIRS OF LIFE.
THERE'S NO PROBLEM SO GREAT SHE
CAN'T SOLVE; HOW TO HOLD YOUR JOB,
HOW TO SUCCEED—CALLS YOUR
FREINDS AND ENEMIES BY NAME
WITHOUT ASKING YOU A SINGLE WORD
& REUNITES THE SEPERATED. COME SEE
ME TODAY. TOMORROW MAY BE TO LATE!

Golden words. REUNITES THE SEPERATED.
Gems!

A little misspelling here and there, but then
God would only send his messages through simple
people who believed, not through scoffers and wise-
guys.

Centered, erect and immobile on a great oak
armchair set up on a dais well in front of the curtained booth, straight and stern as a prophet should
be, sat the proprietress, Princess Zoe.

Her plump dark hands rested on the wooden
arms of the chair. Her strong blunt fingers caressed
the carved scroll at the front of each arm. Her painted
fingernails, so long they curved over the front of her
fingers, hooked into the wood.

Momma stared at the arms, at the strong hands
and the flat fingers with their dreadful painted cres-
cents, and then she looked up and was trapped—

magnetized—by the power in the intense dark eyes that challenged her from the stony face hooded by the scarlet sequined kerchief.

They were somber knowing eyes.

Blacker than all blackness.

They penetrated to the infinite truth.

What a strong face, so swarthy and bold.

What a royal distinguished nose!

Momma clutched her small purse to her chest. Here was power beyond the human.

Princess Zoe was the real thing.

She was a rendezvous with destiny, all right, in her gorgeous low-necked blouse and her ropes of gold coins and those enormous gleaming pendant earrings.

She inclined her head slightly and closed her eyes.

Her head remained fixed, tilted in its rather enigmatic position. Opening her eyes to find Momma transfixed, she raised her hand and beckoned slowly, ever so slowly, with a jeweled forefinger.

"No!" Momma shook her head vigorously.

The fortuneteller continued to gaze into Momma's face, her solemn liquid eyes wide with sadness.

Such strength and power was in this gaze that Momma began to tremble. With difficulty she kept control of herself. Her bladder was weak this last year and sometimes betrayed her—she wore two pair of woollies even on warm days—but she couldn't, she mustn't, let that happen here, now, where this seer would know her childish shame.

Momma moved her feet so they were close together her thighs pressing one against the other.

She had always had a great sense of personal dignity and most of it depended upon control of her own body. Her elementary school teachers on the East Side had stressed continence and cleanliness as the basis of good character. They had worked magic changing greenies' children into Americans. Why, people hearing Momma speak often thought she was quite educated.

Schools in those days were really schools. They knew what to teach.

The fortuneteller sat there unmoving, unblinking.

After all, what did Sol know?

A factory worker, a piece-worker. More than forty years in America and still he had not been able to get rid of his accent.

He was not capable of recognizing the truth that there are special people with the rare gift of sight into the unseeable.

Blessed are Thou, O Lord, whose mercy gives us special magic. Amen.

Momma often composed little prayers of her

own.

Judaism, great as it was, and it was very great, was unfair to women. The morning prayer with its bitter line: *Blessed art Thou, O Lord our God! King of the Universe, who has not made me a woman*—that always rankled her. Sure, women had their own line to say, and there was an explanation, but she wasn't fooled. There was always an explanation. Men were good with the words.

But they didn't know it all. If in their inadequacy they failed to formulate prayers for certain occasions, Momma would just make up her own. What harm could it do to talk directly to God?

Sol was, after all, an unexceptional man. A good man but what could she expect from him?

Closing her eyes to free herself from the gaze of the sphinx, Momma turned toward the other window and then limped over to it.

She came face-to-face with the enormous India-ink drawing on white pasteboard, a human head with wiggly lines delineating broad areas of it the way simple maps are marked for children.

She had to step back to read the legend.

Nervously, she felt for her forehead and the top of her head, anxious fingertips touching and exploring the three deep worry furrows that divided her brow and rested like strata on the tiny frown hollows extending up from her nose. The front of the skull contained the intellectual powers, the perceptive powers, the moral powers. All the good qualities were located in the forehead and top-front of the head.

Like an eager Braille reader, she got much pleasure from what her fingertips transmitted.

A high forehead meant superiority.

She'd heard that many times but here was scientific proof.

Never mind that her forehead made her face too large. Never mind that in her younger years she had worn the glossy black hair in a variety of dips and puffs to conceal some of the mannishly broad expanse of brow.

Now her hair was short and choppy—home cut—and the forehead was bare for all to see.

Perhaps the fortuneteller had a copy of this fine phrenology drawing. How nice it would be to keep in the linen drawer with Ben's birth certificate and elementary school diploma.

Sol kept stuffing all the clumsy outsized mail from Washington in the drawer, but, never mind, she would throw it all out one day soon.

Printed condolences—not worth the fancy paper they were printed on.

Running up to the door of the shop, she grabbed the handle and pushed. A cowbell ribboned onto the inner knob pealed loudly at the movement of the door.

The fortuneteller rose. Surprisingly, she was quite short and squat. She tipped forward slightly on her high-heeled golden sandals, a splendid ominous creature. The silver scales of her blouse shimmered as they caught the light.

"Can you tell me why I'm here?" Momma held tight to the door keeping it safely open. "Please, can you tell me why I'm here?"

Princess Zoe clasped her hands across her waist and gazed downward taking in, first, the arthritic stance of Momma's right foot with its arched ankle and then the shabby polished shoes with run-down heels. She shut her basilisk eyes.

"Someone is missing."

"Oh God!"

The fortuneteller stepped down to move in closer and gaze ravenously at Momma's face. "Your son!"

"No!" Momma screamed, and she pushed the door open to run into the sun-warmed street.

"Your son!" the fortuneteller repeated triumphantly, following Momma through the doorway, and then she stood watching her limping flight.

When the frightened figure hesitated at the end of the street then turned the corner instead of crossing, Zoe entered the store and resumed her seat.

FOUR

Midday, Sol left the dim comfort of the quiet deserted shul to walk the eight blocks home to see if Momma was back.

He hurried along the broken Williamsburg pavements, past the cracked stoops and the occasional small stores, past the massive YMCA building, that impenetrable corner fortress with its *lumpen* young men always hanging around on the steps eyeing Jewish girls.

On he moved, past the public library, an island of peace in the bubbling populous sea, where—incredibly—all the Hungarian and Yiddish newspapers were available if a man only had the time.

He came to Eastern District High School, the school Ben had hated so, and he averted his eyes from the bitterness of the sight.

He wondered at himself.

He had traveled so far across an ocean, and then somehow he had been stopped at the Williamsburg Bridge.

Why? How?

He could not say. He was not good at puzzles.

Going along as quickly as he could, he followed—without noticing—his usual route home.

He arrived at Lee Avenue, the shopping street with its markets and small hammer-on-the-head stores. Credit? Eternally by the week. Fixed prices? Unheard of. Plenty of ragged brown paper bills on poverty's long spikes.

Why hadn't he picked up and gone, invented something, done something, tried his luck somewhere else?

Momma was always clipping items out of the *Reader's Digest* for him to read, items about big successes by small people. She still clung to the foolish remnant of hope from her girlhood reading: Horatio Alger stories. Her American teachers had taught her to dream.

But he?

He knew better.

Life was to be accepted, and clung to, not challenged.

He moved past the basement butcher shop and the tiled, well-lit delicatessen.

The Russian barber, straddling a chair on the sidewalk beside his pole, eyed passers-by critically. At Sol, he scowled severely. Time for a haircut, Sol knew.

On he walked, past the white-curtained Chinese Hand Laundry and then past Cheap Simon, the Notions Man. Simon labored outdoors building pyramids like his ancestors had done. Only Simon's pyramids were of Scot tissues and Lux Soapflakes. Easier than bricks without straw, Sol liked to kid him. The Jews had come a long way.

Sol nodded to Simon.

"Mr. Greenfield. Yoo-hoo! Mr. Greenfield—wait!"

The small bent woman, shrouded from shoulders to ankles in a stiff white apron, jumped up from the bench in front of Stein's Appetizing and grabbed Sol's arm.

As usual she was as immaculate as a surgeon, graying hair pulled back in a bun, face scrubbed-looking, steel-rimmed eyeglasses sitting low on her nose, skin as shriveled as the olives she sold.

Through the store's open door came the spicy aromas of pickles and sour tomatoes and endless varieties of herring.

"So long it's been since you were in my store, I wasn't sure you were you already, I wasn't sure am I maybe calling out to a strange man?"

He paused reluctantly. "Take my word. It's me. So how are you, Mrs. Stein?"

"Should I complain? You wouldn't have time enough to listen. Nobody ever does. Come. Sit down a minute. I have time. My sons-in-law, they're wonderful. They run the whole store. 'Sit outside in the sun, Ma,' they tell me." She patted the bench beside her. "You, too, sit a minute," she urged. "Sit here."

Against his better judgment, he sat.

"You're such a religious man these days," she observed. "My husband tells me that night and day you're in the shul?"

The woman had the right tongue for a fishwife.

"I can't stay, Mrs. Stein."

"Sit, sit. I know your wife such a long time. Sit and talk a minute with an old friend."

A lie. She had never been a friend because Momma wouldn't pay her prices for belly lox and whitefish, not while on Havemeyer Street, a half-mile away, the same fish—better fish—could be bought after a little haggling for half the price.

Momma and Mrs. Stein had battled over prices so fiercely that their relationship was reduced to grim nods now whenever they came face to face.

Momma preferred to take the roundabout route home so she wouldn't have to pass the appetizing store with Mrs. Stein lurking on the bench out front. Avoidance and not-speaking were Momma's favorite combat techniques.

Ordinarily, Sol despised such childishness, but in the case of Mrs. Stein he could understand it.

She was nobody's friend.

Now she was inventing an intimacy with them because they had a tragedy and she found that tragedy exciting.

"I'm so sorry about your Ben. He was a good boy not like some of them around here. You heard they broke my window with a baseball? Right into the half-sours went their home run and the glass fell like rain."

She rocked in mourning for the lost pickles.

"But your son was a nice boy. He used to help his momma carry the bundles all the time. You have a good wife she should live till a hundred ten years. She shlepps five miles to save a penny."

She made a sucking sound as if a cork had just been popped from her mouth.

"I always say a person shouldn't worry so for pennies. Aigh—" Her sigh was an elegy to unsold high-priced appetizing. "You had any news?"

"The army says he's missing."

"The army? My enemies should all be in the army. The baseballniks who broke my window, they should be in the army. Not a fine young boy like your son."

"He wanted to go."

Mrs. Stein poked a shriveled finger under her eyeglasses and rubbed her eye.

"God should only help him."

This piety was automatic, like a *gesundheit*

called out by a stranger, carrying no thought or meaning.

Horrified, Sol sensed a wetness in his own eyes, and he rose immediately. He would not cry with this crocodile.

"*He* should help you too, Mrs. Stein, with the baseballniks and the pickles—with everything. He should only help us all."

He hurried around the corner and down Grant Street past grubby children and their heavy mothers sitting spread-kneed on stoops.

Then, carefully, he tiptoed around a tiny grandmother, her eyes shut, her face a yellow, shriveled rose; she was set out on a canvas beach chair in the middle of the sidewalk, airing like a baby on the beach. She had slept this way, afternoons, next to the Greenfield stoop ever since Sol could remember, a frail enduring monument to the loyalty of her children and the tenacity of life.

She was an inspiration, Momma said.

What kind of inspiration?

She was old so she slept all the time.

Momma made too much of these things.

He climbed the three flights of stairs in the darkness, and then he paused for breath in the shabby hall outside his own door.

The aura of the place settled over him at once: yellow soap, old clothes, the smell of cabbage, dark evenings and cold mornings, many memories of pain and despair.

Along with a young boy's noisy laughter.

All were present here in the musty hall.

His life was entombed here, his and Momma's, and now Ben's.

He turned the knob.

Locked.

He knocked, and then he knocked again.

Where could she be so long?

"Momma? Momma, are you inside? Momma—it's Sol."

No answer came.

He took out his key, but before using it he stooped and peeked through the keyhole. His crazy imagination.

No one.

Entering, he walked through the rooms unable to keep himself from opening the big closet to search inside and from looking under the beds.

No one.

She simply was not back yet.

He locked the door and went slowly down the stairs deciding to walk the round-about route so that he wouldn't have to pass Stein's again.

Don't worry, he told himself. Don't be foolish. Momma's all right.

It's just a very hard day.

She must be all right.
Orthodox Jews dasn't commit suicide.
She knows that.

FIVE

"I've been waiting for you."

The fortuneteller held the door wide open, the bell clapper pinched silent between her painted talons.

Past her, Momma rushed, past her and into the store, and, covering her face with her hands, Momma began to pray fervently.

She remembered to move one hand up from her eyes to the top of her head to replace the missing head scarf. Peering through splayed fingers, she noted that the seer was absolutely still. Indeed, she seemed to have stopped breathing.

Those great eyes were fixed—on Momma?

No—past Momma.

Past walls, buildings, cities, continents, through darkness and the great void, finally into the light. The fortuneteller was seeing all, grasping all, realizing the great and infinite truth.

"I see—" she intoned, her awesome low voice piercing Momma's heart as surely as the voice of God must have pierced Abraham's so long ago—"*missing*"—

She clasped her hands compassionately. "Lost."

Immediately, Momma sensed that she was in a presence that transcended the ordinary. Her mind disengaged, floated free as a bubble.

Weak with relief, she understood that the fortuneteller was seeing all.

Seoul. Pusan. Taejon. Sinch'on. Kaesong. Panmunjom.

Strange cities in a strange land. Strange people.

Mud and war.

And blood.

Surely she would help Momma to peer into that far-off mystery.

"One of your beloved children," the seer murmured.

"I don't have any others," Momma said apologetically.

A magnificent nostril twitched disdainfully.

"Your only beloved son!"

Momma would have embraced her. She would have screamed or keeled over in a faint except that she was frozen by the fear that all this would disappear and it would be Black Sunday in Williamsburg again.

Sagging at the knees, she was immediately

aided by the fortuneteller who moved in solicitously and took her arm and gave her support.

Princess Zoe's strong fingers slid forward from the huddled elbow to the wrist of the hand clutching the small purse. Momma transferred it to her other hand as the Princess began purposefully to lead her into the soft draped darkness of the fortunetelling booth set up behind the chair.

"You cry here," she advised, using both her hands to maneuver Momma in and seat her.

She helped Momma onto a wooden kitchen chair which was really the only sort of chair for a woman Momma's age wearing a boned corset.

Upholstered chairs were always such an embarrassment.

Princess Zoe's clean windows and her hard chair were proofs of integrity. These and the glittering sign pinned to the curtain above Momma—GOD IS LOVE—were all reassuring.

After dropping the entrance curtain, Princess Zoe brought a three-legged stool—so low it looked like a milking stool—and seated herself on it, facing Momma.

At Zoe's elbow was a small end table on which stood a statue of the Virgin, and, in front of it, a red votive candle in a glass. The Princess lit the candle.

The flickering yellow wisp was the only light in the curtained tent.

"Rest as long as you like," Princess Zoe urged gently.

Taking up Momma's right hand, she turned it palm upward and began to stroke it, to smooth it repeatedly and to study what she read there in the abused cracked skin.

Momma began to babble.

"You're very kind, too kind. Really, I don't know how to thank you."

Sobbing, she pressed the useless handkerchief to her chafed nose.

"The Lord will remember you and reward you. I was led here today, you know. I'm a lucky woman because I got another chance. The Lord is good to me."

The stroking continued in unbroken rhythm. "Tell me. Tell me all."

Momma's weeping abated.

During the past year she had wept often but briefly each time the sadness closed in on her. Her tears were like the twilight storms during the terrible New York summers, heaviness before then quick in their passage leaving no relief.

Afterward, only discomfort remained.

"I was blessed. Long long after the first marriage years when young women bear children—at the time when I was already facing change-of-life—God smiled on me as he smiled on Sarah and to me he gave a son.

"I was old enough to be a grandmother when I weaned my baby. He was a gift to me for my old age. God forgot about me until it was almost too late, but then he remembered me generously."

"God is just," Zoe affirmed.

"Mine was the most beautiful baby anyone ever saw, ten pounds four ounces and not wrinkled and red and ugly like other boy babies.

"He was so beautiful that I couldn't walk a single block pushing the carriage that some woman shouldn't come up to me and say what an angel, what a darling, where did I get such a child?

"I didn't walk once on Lee Avenue that some gossip shouldn't remark how sturdy he looked—but I always spat three times to save him from the evil eye. I always took care. Always."

Momma paused, frightened.

"Is it possible I missed one time, and I neglected to spit so this happened? This whole year I've thought about that. I honestly can't remember such a thing.

"He was so good, so fine you can't imagine, and I cared for him, oh how I cared for him, night and day, because that's what a mother is.

"And now THEY say he is missing.

"THEY say he may even be dead.

"Why? Just because they found his few belongings. They shipped home a belt and a camera and letters I wrote him and twenty-seven Oriental coins he was collecting.

"This they send home to a mother? Here is what's left of your son?

"No! He is not dead." Momma turned her wet fevered face into the shadows. "I don't believe it. I didn't see him dead."

"There there, dear, you are a good woman, a very good woman," Princess Zoe crooned as she stroked, her hand moving with practiced gentleness. "It's all right, dear."

"Almost every night he comes to me in my mind and he's alive," Momma declared passionately. "He's real. He's more real than you are now, Princess."

A small spasm jerked through the fortuneteller's body but she did not look up. She had begun to study the lines in Momma's palm and she appeared intent on what she saw.

"I see him. true as life, standing tall and straight as a young tree. He's wearing his *talis,* the prayer shawl with the fringes, that Sol gave him for his bar mitzvah, and in his hand is a prayer book and he's pleading with me, 'Momma, don't forget me. I don't eat *trayf* meat and I pray when I can. Don't let them bury me, Momma. I think of your cooking, your potato pudding and your stuffed cabbage, Momma.

Save me, Momma, it's up to you.'"

"Yes!" Princess Zoe echoed, "It is up to you!"

"It's up to me," Momma mumbled and slumped low in the chair.

"I'll bring you a drink of water, dear. Rest. You have suffered too much." Zoe slipped through the layered cloths at the back of the tent leaving Momma collapsed like a drunkard on her chair.

"Here is a glass of *clean* water. "It is fresh and clean as could be."

Momma reached for the glass, hesitated, then decided against it, withdrawing her hand. "No, thanks. I'm sorry I behaved so badly. I never let myself go this way."

"The water is clean, dear. I scrubbed the glass myself with Rocake's powder."

Momma had to smile at the mispronunciation of the kosher brand name.

Noting the smile, Princess Zoe bristled. "You see, I know you're Jewish."

Infatuated by this clairvoyance, Momma now grabbed the glass and drank. "How did you know?" She dabbed at the corners of her mouth with her handkerchief.

"I know everything."

Taking back the glass, Princess Zoe set it on the floor and then she picked up Momma's hand and once again began to study it. "How lucky you are that you came here today, dear," she murmured. "What's your name?"

"Momma—I mean Eva, Eva Greenfield. But when my son was born, my joy was so great everyone began to call me Momma, and that's what I'm called to this day—Momma."

"Now let me see your other hand."

The fortuneteller concentrated on the left palm for a while then glanced from one hand to the other comparing findings.

When she spoke again, her words were measured, slow and sonorous with meaning. She kept her voice low. "You are so lucky. I don't want to scare you, but you better pray to the Jewish God tonight. I'll pray to him too and burn the candle all night."

This proposed devotion made Momma uncomfortable, but she said nothing. She looked down at her hands, their cracked fingers and scarred skin barely visible in the dark tent. Timidly she asked, "What is it you see?"

First, the fortuneteller shook her head. Then she whispered cautiously. "I can't say. It is something terrible. An evil force is after you and what happens now is all up to me. If I make one false move—" She ran her forefinger straight as a razor across her throat—"Ggggh."

Momma clutched her own throat. "What is

it?"

"I see shadows in your lines. I am not allowed to say what I see. But I understand your terrible problems and I have to deal with them. You must not worry; now it's all up to me."

The sequined head moved very close to Momma's ear.

"You have other work to do. You will go home now. Next Friday morning at ten o'clock, you must go to the bank and take out a hundred dollars—see they give you a nice fresh crisp bill, not a dirty piece of cabbage. Then take it home and hide it.

"On Saturday night once it's good and dark, I want you to go and buy a fresh egg—and also buy a large white man's handkerchief, the best quality. Take them home. Get out two woolen blankets and put them on your bed. Then you get under those blankets and take the egg and hold it on your navel with both your hands cupping it. When the egg is very warm, I want you to wrap it in the hundred dollar bill and tie it up in the new handkerchief and hide it in your closet.

"Early Sunday morning I want you to take a warm bath. You must be very clean. After you have washed, lie back in the water and go over every single step you took. See if you followed all my directions."

Zoe sat up abruptly, her expression very severe.

"If you didn't do it all right, forget it. I'll be of no use to you. If you did everything right then bring the bundle to me.

"Can you remember all that?" she demanded.

Momma nodded vehemently. How could she possibly forget the formula for life?

"I am helping you because I like you. I feel sorry for you and your troubles. People like me with special powers are on this earth to do good things for friends. You are a good mother, I can tell. I don't want you to pay me a single cent, not now or ever. I work side-by-side with the spirits. No money allowed.

"But I must warn you if you say one word about this—to the bank clerk or your husband or *anyone* you'll make the spirits angry. Then I won't be able to help you. Your boy's life will be in danger.

"You better not let that happen."

"Not a soul will know," Momma vowed.

"Put your right hand on your heart," Zoe ordered, "and swear it on your son's life."

Momma was trembling. She could barely pick her hand up. "I swear—I swear on Ben's life. Oh! When will he come?"

"Trust me. You have suffered too much already."

Princess Zoe stood up and pulled back the

entrance drape, a heavy maroon hanging edged with tiny pompoms. The sudden light streaming in made Momma blink.

She rose and smoothed her skirt. "Good-bye, Princess Zoe. I'll do exactly as you say. I'll be prompt next Sunday. You can count on me to be here really early. Thank you for all you are doing."

"Don't thank me. I'm helping you because you need a friend. We spiritualists are put here to do good things for friends. To help. Like my sign says—" she pointed to the cardboard pinned up above on the cloth wall—"GOD IS LOVE!"

SIX

Sunday, May 20, 1951

Excitement woke Momma before six and rather than just lie there listening to the window's steady rattle, she decided to take her bath. Baths were ordinarily once-a-week affairs, Friday evenings before sundown. But today was an extraordinary day; special cleanliness was necessary. She had been warned.

Hushing the squealing faucets, Momma ran the bath then cautiously climbed in. She soaped herself and lay back in the warm water. She would go over every step and check and double check to be sure she had followed all of Zoe's instructions. All week her mind had stayed as alert as a detective's, paying particular attention to everything she had done.

Soaping herself vigorously first, she then closed her eyes and gave herself up to the ease offered by the tepid water.

Her review started with the narrow escape

she'd had Friday morning at the bank. Mr. Morse, her regular teller, when he'd heard her say "Withdrawal" and seen the slip, actually dropped his eyeglasses. You'd think it was *his* money she was asking for. Luckily, the glasses were fastened to a black lace around his neck so they didn't shatter.

"You want to take money out?"

"Yes, Mr. Morse. I want a fresh clean hundred dollar bill."

Opening the bankbook, he noted what they both already knew, that this was her first withdrawal. There was a stiff cleanness to the pages; the printed similar sums and dates marched side by side, infantry rows down the white field. All had been inviolate until now.

"It's for something wonderful, Mr. Morse—"

He nodded and, turning his back, he set the book in the machine. Hand poised to punch the keys, he turned his head once more toward her. "Withdrawal? You're sure?"

"Yes." She was annoyed with him. Did he think she was an ignoramus? "Withdrawal, Mr. Morse. Withdrawal."

Without further delay he punched away at the machine, and when, finally, he handed the violated bankbook to her, the money was sandwiched in it.

"Enjoy your day."

"You, too." Momma did her best to be gracious. "Thank you."

The crisp bill was clean and without even a center crease. She'd had to fold it once to get it in her pocket, but she'd ironed the fold out as soon as she reached home. Then she hid the money in the couch where it lay now, flat and safe.

Better not to let anyone know her business. From now on when she had money to deposit, she would go to the other teller. Mr. Morse was a nice man, but he knew too much about her savings. It was unfortunate that she'd have to avoid him now, because he'd always been very cordial, even when her deposits were only half-dollars during the bad times. Yes, she would certainly go to the other teller's window after this.

Momma interrupted her reverie and turned on the hot water. The bath had grown cold.

Saturday had crept by as if each hour were being held back.

Breakfast.

Clean up.

Lunch.

Clean up.

At four, finally, Sol had started for shul. He'd been so jumpy all day, she was glad to see him go off for evening prayers. For the whole week she'd been awaiting this miraculous night, and it seemed to her that sundown was arbitrarily slow in arriving. For a while she sat trying to read the *Daily News*. Such bold underwear ads. Was there no modesty left in the world?

She paged through the paper slowly, stopping at pictures of new brides. Why did they always show the bride and not the groom? All pretty, happy-looking girls. Poor things, they did not know what lay ahead.

When she could barely make out the print on her newspaper, Momma checked the clock again but it was still fifteen minutes before the time the Jewish calendar specified for turning on the lights. The Williamsburg Savings Bank must have calculated their calendars for Jews living at the North Pole. Even a blind man could see that it was night already in Brooklyn. Trust banks to make Jewish calendars.

There wasn't enough in the newspapers to keep her busy till sundown. She refolded the pages neatly so the front page was on top. One thing had to be said for the *News* and the *Post*. They were a handy size.

War headlines.

She averted her eyes from them.

Nothing really to read in the newspaper.

She went to the grocery carton in the hall to look at the eggs there.

No.

Princess Zoe had specifically said a *fresh* egg

and a *new* handkerchief. These were good eggs but not good enough.

Again she had to sit, and she looked out the window at the run-down yards below, at the great oak tree that was her comfort because she thought of it as Nature and Nature was good.

This had been a better week than she had had all year. Before last Sunday she had been helpless, a victim. It wasn't the first time Fate had blighted her life. In the autumn of 1929 right after she broke a hand-mirror, Sol lost his job and disaster fell upon on her family and haunted them for years afterward.

But this time, Princess Zoe would intercede for her.

Serenity came with this knowledge. And optimism. If only she'd known Princess Zoe in the 1930's, she thought wistfully. If only....

Sundown.

She washed her face and put on a light gray jacket, took up her brown paper shopping bag and, after reaching under the couch mattress to ascertain that the hundred dollar bill was in place, she locked up and went about her errands.

First step, the TUDOR-STUART HABER-DASHERY on Roebling Street, a splendid store with a red neon gentleman in white tie and tails as its sign. Momma had never been inside here before. She knew that in a fancy shop the customer paid the rent.

However, it was necessary today because this was the best men's shop in Williamsburg.

"Yes, Madame?" The thin balding proprietor advanced from behind the counter decorously, his every movement studied. His life was dedicated to dispensing Fruit of the Loom underwear with extreme unction. "How are you this Sabbath night? What can I do for you?"

"I want a man's handkerchief." Momma lifted her hand to pat her hair in place. "A fine white handkerchief, please."

"Yes, Madame. White is always dressy."

Taking down two great black cardboard boxes, he blew the dust from their covers then opened them and unfolded one handkerchief from each.

Momma appraised both handkerchiefs. After wiping her hand on her jacket, she rubbed the fabric of each between thumb and forefinger, testing for texture. Both were good quality. God only knew what he would ask. On Havemeyer Street, handkerchiefs were ten cents each and sometimes twelve for a dollar.

"I only want the best," she declared.

"I only carry the best, Madame." His tone was a reprimand.
"This is not Havemeyer Street. I sell to big people, the biggest. Abe Stark, himself, bought jockey shorts here from me more than once."

Momma blushed. "How much are you asking?"

"This model with the white-on-white border is thirty-five cents. The plain white is on special sale today at twenty-five cents."

Your name is *goniff?* Momma was sorely tempted to ask. My name is Greenfield, not Rockefeller. She locked her teeth stifling the impulse to haggle. He was a crook, but this was not the right time to confront him. She would take the white-on-white.

But suppose it wasn't right? Princess Zoe wouldn't be able to help her.

Momma couldn't chance it. She stood staring at the handkerchiefs unable to choose.

Her decision was reckless. "I'll take them both."

She would let the fortuneteller decide which one was more appropriate and then she would give the other one to Sol. His handkerchiefs were rags already. This extra one need not go to waste. Momma felt happy, lighthearted in her extravagance. At last, she was *doing* something.

"Please put them in a gift box. They're for a very special purpose."

He hesitated.

"I am buying *two.*"

Biting his lip, Mr. Tudor-Stuart reached up

high on a shelf and brought down a flat shiny square of cardboard which folded into a box.

"That's fine," Momma approved. "Maybe with a small sheet of tissue inside to keep them from wrinkling?"

He complied, silently.

Momma was proud of herself for not being intimidated.

In her brother Ike's store, THE EGGERY—he had made up the name himself—Momma had to wait her turn. She looked over all the different kinds of eggs. The various grades were displayed in bins beneath the glass counter: small, medium, large, browns and whites. Carefully set aside in a bowl were the "crack-eggs," which went for less money because they were slightly damaged by hairline cracks.

Maybe Ike would be suspicious.

Maybe she should have gone to strangers, to another store.

But she never bought eggs elsewhere. How could she be sure of the quality?

Ike gave her the usual noisy hello. "Look, look, look who's here. What can I do for you, Big Sister?"

"Hello, Ike. I want one egg, one large, beautiful egg. It should be fresh, the freshest you have in stock. Give me the best egg in your whole store."

Ike's mouth hung open as he stared at her. He was a large, soft, red-faced man, this younger brother of hers, and she could usually tell what he was thinking. Right now he was thinking he had heard wrong.

"One-single-large-grade A-egg?" he questioned? "You're giving a small party?"

Always with the jokes. Momma had tried time and again to forgive Ike for his crudeness and for his unsuitable marriage—but she could not. He was a good soul and during the hard days when they were hungry he had helped them. If only he were not such a clown.

Still, a brother was a brother.

"No party, Ike. I just need a specially good egg."

Momma peered around nervously and was relieved that her sister-in-law, Fanny, was not in the store at the moment. Fanny was selfish. She did not like Ike to save the crack-eggs for his sister. First-come first-served, was her slogan; whatever customer wanted them should get them.

Once Momma had been witness to a terrible family argument during which Fanny had shouted at Ike, "You want to give eggs, give whole eggs. Don't knock them under the counter then say they're crack-eggs."

Of course, Momma had resolved right then and there never to enter Ike's store again, but Ike swore and swore that Fanny's words were not true and that Momma was helping him out by taking the damaged eggs off his hands.

"How are you?" Ike asked. "Where's Sol?"

"I'm all right. And Sol is in shul. How is Fanny?" She wasn't really interested, but she asked out of politeness.

"Fine, fine. She's in the beauty parlor, her regular Saturday night appointment: shampoo, setting, nails. The works."

Momma nodded.

"Listen," Ike said, "I'll give you the very best egg in the store. But what about the crack-eggs I saved for you? I put eight aside. You don't want them?"

Momma considered. She did need more eggs. And Princess Zoe had *not* said she couldn't buy other things when she came out for the special items.

What harm could it do?

"I'll take the crack-eggs too, Ike. But please pack them separately. The Grade A egg give me in a little bag."

Ike nodded.

Ceremoniously he moved his hand, fingers arched, back and forth over the white eggs until he settled on a large one. It was, after all, the first of its kind in her history. Wrapping it carefully in a sheet of newspaper, he then inserted that packet in a small bag. For the crack-eggs, he used an egg carton tying top and bottom together securely.

Momma, nodding approval at all he was doing, relented in her judgment of him. Ike was a diamond in the rough. But a diamond!

Home again, she hid the secret purchases then put together two Swiss cheese sandwiches on rye bread for Sol and one on whole wheat bread for herself. They always took a light supper on the Sabbath.

From the top of the clothes closet she lugged a massive cardboard carton in which the winter blankets were camphored. Pulling out two fuzzy gray blankets, she shook them out the window. The odor of camphor filled the room.

As soon as he came in, Sol began to sniff, and then he saw the blankets. "Why are the woolen blankets out, Mom?"

"I'm cold."

"In the middle of May, the warmest May in years?"

"I'm cold, I said. Can't I be cold if I want to?"

"Be cold. Be hot. Be whatever you like."

He ate the sandwiches and drank his coffee reading his newspaper as usual.

Momma remained in the kitchenette. She ate standing up, looking out at the great leafy tree in the yard. Glancing in at Sol from time to time, she wondered, what was there so much to read?

That evening was the longest of her life.

"I think I'll pack it in," he said, at last.

Thank God. He was going.

Carefully, she made up her own bed with the two winter blankets. Then she undressed, all except for her slip. Tiptoeing to the linen closet, she dug out the handkerchiefs and the egg from under the pile of old pillowcases. She listened for Sol's breathing. It was regular. He wasn't snoring yet, but she'd take a chance. Once he went to bed, he never rose till morning. It was she who had heard Ben's childhood cries, the mice scratching and scampering, and all the other night noises through the years.

The white-on-white handkerchief was all she took from the box; the other could just stay folded inside. She would carry both to Coney Island just in case.

She pulled the light cord then moved soundlessly back to the couch, slid the hundred dollar bill out from under, and, holding the three precious items before her, she clumsily got onto the couch.

Lying flat on her back, she put the bill and the handkerchief beside her on the mattress, and she held the egg pressed against her navel. In the darkness the shell felt cool and smooth. more like a fragile precious stone than an egg. Closing her eyes, she breathed in deeply. How marvelous that an egg should help! And how right. A child began as an egg. Ben was part of her; that was why it hurt so much. Ben had been tied to that navel that was now working a miracle for him. God moved in mysterious ways His wonders to perform.

Eggs were remarkable; she'd always loved them: poached, fried, soft-boiled, scrambled, in French toast, in meat loaf, or best of all mashed with chicken livers and onion.

The cantor in the shul drank raw eggs to improve his voice.

All the nutritionists recommended eggs.

If an egg had a blood spot, even if you were starving you had to throw it out. Some non-Jews used bloody eggs which only showed how much sense *they* had.

Children loved baby chicks at Easter-time.

Not only chickens came from eggs but all sorts of creatures: alligators, turtles, frogs, and where had she read once that the male catfish carried all the fertilized eggs in his mouth for more than two months and didn't eat in all that time until the eggs were hatched. *That* was being a good father. What that must taste like! And how difficult to remember not to swallow.

Orientals buried eggs in the ground for years and then ate them rotten. That was even worse than blood spots. Poor Ben, to have to go and fight in a war with such barbarians. Who knew what he had to eat?

She was sweating; she could feel the coating of wetness on her neck and shoulders. With high blood pressure she was always too warm, and now under the blankets it was cruelly hot. Still she lay covered wanting to do what was exactly right.

The egg rested in the flaccid flesh of her belly.

She thought of Ben coming home and of how happy they would be.

She was arranging it all.

The egg was warm. Momma took up the hundred dollar bill and rolled the egg in it then covered it with the white-on-white handkerchief and wrapped the whole thing up neatly using her belly as table. Gently, she lifted the cloth packet off and, getting up, padded to the closet to bury it in the nest of soft linens. She set the box containing the extra handkerchief as a marker so she would know where to dig, and then she covered the whole pile with more small linens.

"Tonight I will rest in peace," she congratulated herself as she returned to bed.

And she slept soundly through all of Saturday night.

Like a child.

***

Now, insistent knocking at the bathroom door roused Momma from her delicious bath torpor.

"What's the matter in there?" Sol demanded. "Maybe another person has to go?"

"Don't clop so on the door. I'll be out in two minutes. I'm taking a bath."

Again with the water. He despaired.

"A new idea in America, a bath on Sunday morning when everyone needs to use the bathroom. What's the matter, you worked so hard on *Shabbos* you're dirty already?"

Momma pulled up the stopper and the rushing water muted his grumbling.

Everything was in order for Princess Zoe.

Everything.

Momma had forgotten nothing.

The Princess could certainly count on her!

SEVEN

Wonders, wonders, Sol thought, on seeing his brother-in-law Ike in shul before him. It was true that Momma's unnecessary bath this morning had made him much later than usual. Still, Ike's religion did not usually assert itself till after the busiest store hours. His being here meant that Fanny had to give up her Sunday morning in bed reading the *Daily News* comics and lazying over her brunch. Fanny was very American in her language and in her diet too. Momma swore she couldn't spend more than five minutes in Fanny's kitchen because of the stench of bacon.

So what? Wasn't America the land of the 57 varieties? At least. There were the kosher-bacon Jews and the *trayf*-bacon Jews; there were the egg-roll-only-on-the-paper-plate-in-the-house-Jews. There were even Jews with three sets of dishes: milk dishes, meat dishes, and *trayf* dishes. To say nothing of the lobster and shrimp-salad Jews.

Slipping into the pew beside Ike, Sol put on his *talis*. Ike nodded but did not speak a word. Though he was not at all religious outside of shul, Ike was fanatically observant when there. Within the temple, he tried to make up for lost time; he prayed loudly and he swayed back and forth like a rocking horse. If God were impressionable, Ike would have impressed Him.

Skeptical thoughts about Ike's spiritual life occurred to Sol often, but he kept them to himself. Ike was essentially a kind man and that made him a good Jew. Sol was not his brother-in-law's keeper.

When prayers were finished, Sol said, "I'll keep you company a little on the way to the store, Ike. I'll walk along with you." He moved out into the aisle quickly.

"Fine. I'm glad of your company." Ike came right behind him, and once he'd caught up he said. "Come to the store and I'll give you hot bagels to take home."

Sol shook his head.

Ike repeated the offer, his voice getting louder. "Such bagels you never had, with onions, with poppy seeds, with raisins and cinnamon. They don't leave bagels alone anymore. No more virgin bagels."

He was trying for a laugh, Sol knew, trying hard to chase away sorrow. But Sol, not up to pretending, walked along silently. Both men carefully avoided the loaded trash cans set out for the next collection.

Not a word for blocks. Then, clumsily, as they crossed Marcy Avenue, Sol forced himself to speak. "Ike—I had a letter yesterday."

The Myrtle Avenue Express roared overhead on its way to the bridge and in its rumbling wake Sol added quietly, "He's dead, Ike. He's dead."

Turning his head sharply away, Sol fumbled in his breast pocket.

"I was afraid...." Ike began. "All this time I was afraid, but I didn't believe it. A kid runs off into the army. The first week of a war they shove him into battle, and then he's missing. Missing almost a year. Common sense made me afraid, but I really didn't believe it. I couldn't."

He read the government letter.

"No!" he said, shaking his head. "No, no, no!"

"Yes," Sol took back the letter. He gripped Ike's shoulder, understanding how much Ike wanted to deny it, to comfort him. So many times Ike had helped them: a loan, a holiday food package, cast-off clothing, a ride to the mountains in the summer. But now Ben was dead and for that tragedy Ike could not just put his hand in his pocket. No *things* would help.

"But Eva was in the store last night, Sol. She didn't say a word about it. She was cheerful."

"She's peculiar these days. Don't expect her to make much sense." He paused finding it very difficult to go on. Then he continued. "About this she doesn't know yet. I couldn't tell her. I tried but I couldn't make the words come from my mouth. And I couldn't just hand her the letter. Only God knows what she'll do when she hears this." He stopped and walked the next few steps in silence, and then words burst from him, a storm pouring itself out with wild force.

"I tell you, Ike, I just don't understand. The arguments run through my head night and day and still I don't understand. I repeat them to myself. The war isn't Truman's fault. He's only the president. One man alone doesn't make policies. One man alone doesn't make wars. But he was in such a hurry to move in, to make it bigger, such a hurry with men and guns and planes. Maybe if he were a bigger man, a better statesman—an FDR or a Wilson—but they were war presidents too. To give them credit, they chose better wars. In those wars, at least, men believed. What's to say, Ike? Who is there to hate? They did something to us, this enemy? They sank our ships or bombed our cities? They hurt our people? What did they do to us? Why should I hate them? There are, maybe, mothers and fathers on the other side too?" His mouth worked convulsively. Swallowing, he tried to rid his throat of the intense pain that jammed it.

"They found the—remains—" He spoke the terrible word with the greatest difficulty. "They knew him by his teeth, my Ben." Sol was crying now. "By his crooked teeth that I couldn't afford to put braces on, they identified him. And now they ask me—a nice question for a father—should they bury him there where he died in Korea, or should they send him home?"

"Let him stay, Sol."

"No. He must come home."

"Sol, he's there. What does it matter? Let him rest where he died."

"No. I already decided." A single tear moved slowly down the sunken track of the cheek and stopped at the mouth.

Ike thrust a handkerchief at him.

"A Jew must not lie in a gentile cemetery." Sol was firm. "Ben must have a Jewish funeral. Momma will want it too once she knows."

"It's a mistake, Sol. I don't know if she can make it through a funeral. You just finished telling me how peculiar she's acting already. It will get worse—" Ike stopped himself abruptly. A minute later he mumbled, "You must do whatever you think is right, Sol, whatever you think is right. Can I help with anything?"

Sol offered his hand and Ike pressed it with both his hands.

"We'll manage, Ike. Somehow people manage. Don't worry. I'll go home now. Momma must be waiting."

"Bagels? Let me send some bagels. Something—"

Sol shook his head.

"Yogurt?" Ike called after him. "Delicious. Like ice cream?"

Sol turned the corner and the voice making the offerings was lost.

EIGHT

There was a tapping on the glass of the street door. Zoe heard the timid sounds at once. Like a little bird pecking: peck, peck, peck. Not like a grown person: knock, knock, knock. Zoe went quickly to tend her lonely sparrow.

"How are you, dear?" Sweetly and carefully, she ushered Momma in. "Come right into the *ofisa*." She led the way into the dim tent. "I've thought about you every single day. Have you had any strange burning feelings in your belly?"

"No."

Pleased, the Princess rubbed her hands. "Good. I have worked hard for you all week. There is much evil all around us." Her eyes shifted cautiously, indicating to Momma how close the evil might be.

Momma had to admire her. Today she was bright in an ankle-length full skirt of yellow satin, her bosom bursting out of a bright blue blouse. Heavy gold jewelry and the skyburst of sequins netted into her hair all glowed in the tent's dimness. She was a fairy-tale princess.

Momma offered the brown paper bag "Here—"

"No. I must wash my hands with Rocake's. I don't want to pollute sacred objects. I am in the middle of preparing things inside. Tell me, did you do everything I asked?"

"Yes, Princess Zoe."

"Did you bathe properly this morning?"

"Yes."

"Then sit here quietly till I am finished preparing." Zoe hurried out back.

In the shadowy darkness, Momma held the parcel to her protectively. The acrid sweet smell of old incense offended her nose. Why didn't Zoe open a window? Scents were lovely but they should be dabbed on the wrists and behind the ears not spread all over the house like poison gas.

The fortuneteller was not gone long.

"Here I am with such a bad foot I can hardly walk," Momma marveled, "and yet I made it here. And I got here early! What a mother does for her children, eh? Nothing is too much for them."

"I understand how you feel," Zoe said. Then, slowly, she volunteered, "I have a son."

"Really? Is he here now? I'd like to meet him."

"No, he is not here. No one is allowed here when I am working with the spirits."

"Of course. Does your son go to school?"

"Gypsy children cannot go to school. Their brains are not accustomed to your work. If a Gypsy child goes to school—" she snapped her fingers sharply—"he gets epileptic fits."

"How strange. For Jews, school is everything." Momma's face was bleak again. "Everything. That's where my tragedy started—in school." Overwhelmed, she swallowed hard and then bowed her head.

"You must tell me what happened," Zoe urged.

And Momma told her: how two years before, just about this time in May, an attendance officer had come stomping up the stairs like a Nazi, shouting, "Greenfield? Greenfield?" Momma had run to let him in, recognizing by his rude manner that he was some sort of official. She had always been frightened by authoritative footsteps on her stairs—they were usually bill collectors—and she had opened her door quickly to keep the landlady from hearing.

The truant officer was as mean as he was loud. After slamming the door, he began with the questions? "Greenfield? You got a son Benny?" Opening a messy black notebook, he wet his pinkie and pushed pages. "Ah ha—Greenfield, Benny—three weeks' consecutive absences."

"Oh no." Momma was much relieved. "You have the wrong Greenfield. It's a very common name. My son is in school right now. By the way, his name is Benjamin. We don't like the name Benny. It's not dignified." She smoothed her hair then pulled her apron straight. This was some clerical error. She smiled at the officer. "Why, I pack his lunch every morning. Today he has two hard-boiled egg sandwiches and an apple."

His eyes swept the shabby living room, the scruffy board floor, the decrepit couch and the blistering yellow walls. "You got him working by any chance?"

"He's not even seventeen." Momma was indignant. "He must finish school. Education is everything in America."

The attendance officer scratched the back of his head. Either she was putting on a good act or she was too innocent for Williamsburg. "Just get him into school tomorrow morning and every morning after that, or else—you go to court with him."

"Court? We have never been in court. My son is a good boy. You just made a mistake and I don't hold it against you. Mistakes happen. Greenfield is a very common name. I'll tell him tonight to find out from the school office what the mix-up is."

"Yes, you do that, lady. You just do that."

That terrible night, they questioned Ben.

He *was* the Benny Greenfield.

He hated school.

Even if he got the diploma—even if he stuck it

out—it wouldn't mean anything. The high school was just one giant web of meaninglessness.

The teachers didn't know who he was, and they didn't care anything about him.

He was simply a name on their records to be processed through the institution if he sat out the time.

In his classes were illiterates and bullies, even criminals, all being passed along in the same system. What did it mean?

He wanted to quit school.

He wanted to get a job and earn money so that he could buy things,

What things? What *things* could make a boy want to give up his education?

Many things. Everything. He was tired of being poor.

America was rich!

He was ashamed of the shabby clothes that Momma picked up on bargain tables, clothes that were either too big or too small. All around him people had everything.

What everything? They kept asking him frantically. What everything?

Cameras, portable radios, television sets, racer bicycles, cars—EVERYTHING!

And he had nothing.

He wanted to live.

He wanted a good time.

"Good times!" Sol had screamed at him, Momma frantically weeping and egging him on. "I'll give you good times, you bum, you good-for-nothing. A Jewish boy without education is dirt on this earth. You finished *cheder* and never opened up a Hebrew book after that—and now you don't want to touch an English book either? If you won't go to school then get out of my house."

"All right." In an instant, the boy was lost in the gloom of the hallway. "All right. I'll get out for good."

Momma's face contorted. "He kept his word. He went for good. And I didn't stop him!" Her body shuddered at the memory. "Sol didn't mean it. He was only upset. He loved him too much!"

"Poor dear," Zoe murmured. "You have been through a lot."

"When will he come home, Princess? Will it be soon?" Momma pleaded.

"Very soon. Very very soon," Zoe soothed her. "Let us do our work for him now, quickly. Spread the handkerchief on the floor."

"I have a problem—" Momma began nervously. She so didn't want to appear foolish. "The shop had two good handkerchiefs, a plain white and a white-on-white. I didn't know which would be better, so I bought them both and I brought them along today. Which one shall I use?"

"Oh, you were so wise to bring two. Whiteness is purity; the more purity the better. Spread them both, the plain one on bottom and the other one on top of it."

Bending over with difficulty, Momma did as she was told.

"Put the hundred dollar bill on the right side of the cloth near the edge."

"Face up or face down?"

"Face down. Evil must not be witnessed." Swiftly, Princess Zoe scanned the inside of the tent checking for intruders. "Hand me the egg."

Momma fumbled but Zoe was deft. In a second she had cracked the egg against the side of the small table and emptied it into the handkerchief.

Momma stared down at the floor. Breathing was difficult in the heavy perfumed air.

There—in the white mucous of Ike's Grade A egg—was an eerie greenish blob.

Mold?

Filth?

Some Grade A egg.

She would give Ike. What was this—a joke?

"Move closer," Princess Zoe commanded.

Inching forward to the edge of her chair reluctantly, Momma bent over.

"Closer."

Momma gasped and then could move no more. The thing wriggling there in the egg slime was a tiny devil's head! It had bristly hair and pointed eyebrows all matted and mucousy, clinging to the pallid death-face; its two sharp horns curved downward while its mouth above a small goatee was twisted upward in a vicious grin.

"Dear God—" Jerking back abruptly, Momma shut her eyes. "Dear, dear God!"

What was happening? She had bought the egg from Ike, her own brother. She made a cage of her fingers and peered through to see if it was still there.

It stared back at her; yes, the ugliness of it leered at her.

Nausea rose in her throat and she gagged.

"Come, honey," Princess Zoe summoned softly. "I was right. This proves it." With skill, she lifted the curtain slightly and slid the white cloths with their frightening mess out of sight.

Momma stared at her, dazed. She had nerves of steel to touch a monstrous thing like that and remain calm.

"Let's sit here quietly." Princess Zoe moved close. She took Momma's hand and began to stroke it gently, and, after a while, she sighed.

"What is it? What is it, Princess Zoe?"

"The spirits tell me that you have money in the bank." Her tone was melancholy.

Were there no secrets in the world from this marvelous woman?

"The spirits feel that the money may be cursed. Cursed money can cause bad luck. Your money must be tested."

"How did my money get cursed? It was earned, every penny."

The Princess glowered. "I am not allowed to tell."

"Sorry. How much—" Momma's voice faltered—"how much is needed for the test?"

"Remember, it is only a test. If your money is clean, you get it all back."

Zoe closed her eyes, and Momma understood that she was trying to ascertain the exact sum.

"For this test the spirits require one thousand dollars."

Momma gasped.

"You," Zoe went on firmly, "must withdraw ten one-hundred dollar bills from your bank and bring them to be tested. Next week we will know for sure if *all* your money is cursed. If it is not cursed, of course, you can take it right back to the bank again. Those very same bills."

"One thousand dollars! Oh, Princess Zoe, can you tell me when he'll come? Only tell me when."

"Soon. Very soon. In fact, you must begin to get ready for him. You have to buy him some welcome-home clothes: a pair of shoes, black, size eleven-and-a-half, and two pair of pants, waist forty-two."

"But Princess Zoe, he's not stout."

"The spirits say he has gained many pounds."

"Oh, I'm so glad." Momma clasped her hands happily.

"Wrap the clothing in white tissue paper and tie it with red ribbon. White stands for holiness and red for—"

"Blood," Momma whispered. "Of course." Princess Zoe made good sense. Sure, if a boy was coming home he needed new clothes.

The Princess was a pillar of strength. More. A fortress.

"Don't carry the money anywhere near the clean clothing," Zoe warned.

"Oh no."

"Good. Then it's all arranged."

Momma made no move. She just sat there, relaxed, knees apart, hands and purse loose in the lap of her gray print dress.

"You must go now. You must go so that I can begin my work for you and your boy. Your story has helped me understand exactly what must be done."

"Princess Zoe—" Momma clutched at the fortuneteller's hand convulsively—"you have so much sympathy."

Zoe smiled. "You know what comes with you

next time?"

"One thousand dollars. And new clothing for Ben."

"May God watch over you till you get it safely here. And may He protect your son. May no one spoil the sacred work I do for you."

Momma was joyous. "Oh, Zoe, after a whole life of being a plain ordinary nobody—how wonderful it is, at last, to have a friend with influence!"

NINE

Sunday, May 27, 1951

"Here are the new clothes for him, Zoe."

"Uh uh. Don't hand them to me here," Zoe's tone was a trifle sharp. "Give them to me in the *ofisa*, dear. In the tent. Just one minute." She locked the street door.

"You know something," Momma observed with pleasure, "you and I are both wearing the same clothes we wore the first day we met. You were dressed in that elegant skirt with the silver sequined blouse, and I had on this gray skirt and print blouse. We both seem to favor blouses and skirts, and we put the same ones on on the same days. Maybe we're telepathic or something."

"Did you think I wouldn't know exactly what you're wearing?"

"Oh. You knew last week too?"

"Of course." Zoe was extremely nonchalant about her extraordinary powers. "Come. Time to go inside."

Obediently, Momma followed her into the curtained den. Morning sun never penetrated here; shadow and darkness prevailed masking the day. "I've brought two pairs of good slacks from Ripley and a pair of Tom McCann shoes," Momma chattered, as she settled herself onto her chair. "You're sure you gave me the right sizes, Zoe. They seem very large for my boy."

"You know how boys grow. You won't know him when you see him."

Momma had to laugh. Not know Ben? What could be more impossible? Zoe was a real comedian.

"Here Zoe. Take it."

"No. I can't touch that package. I must go and cleanse myself. This is a bad time for me. I have to be careful what I touch. I am unclean."

Zoe slipped out. Almost at once, she was back.

"What do you mean?" Momma asked, intrigued.

"I am *makhrime*. Bleeding. I am not allowed to touch food or plants."

"But those are Jewish rules," Momma said, astonished. "To keep a woman from handling food or spoiling plants—that is our custom."

"Ours too. A Gypsy woman sleeps alone when she is that way. She doesn't do the cooking. She eats on separate plates, and she keeps herself away from men."

"Zoe," Momma was joyful, "you won't believe it but we have the same rules."

"Of course I believe it. That's how come we can be such close friends, my dear. We're from the same kind of people."

"How right you are. I was just thinking this week how much Gypsies are like Jews—wanderers who don't mix—and then I read a story in the Jewish paper about Hitler and the Gypsies. The same week the idea came into my mind, the Jewish paper wrote about it. Isn't that something?"

"What did the paper write about Gypsies?"

"You mean you don't know?" Momma felt a heightened importance. She hadn't known a thing about it until this article, but now it was vital that her friend know too.

"It's a very sad story, Zoe. A tragedy. You see, Hitler and the Nazis didn't like any people who weren't German. They didn't like wanderers; they believed that everyone should live in his own place. They hated Jews the most, but they hated plenty of others. So the Nazis arrested Gypsies—*Zigeuner* they called them—wherever they marched in Europe, and they marched many places. The Gypsies were put in prison; some were tortured and some were killed. Who knows how many? The newspaper said maybe twenty thousand Gypsies were killed in Hitler's camps," Momma finished sadly.

"It is just a story," Zoe snorted. "Who could kill twenty thousand Gypsies?"

"Hitler killed six million Jews."

"Gypsies are different. We are not *Bibolde*. We are fighters. No one could kill twenty thousand Gypsies, not even your Hitler."

"My Hitler?" Momma spat air. "A *kaporah* on him." Zoe's response bothered her. After all, had she not read it with her own eyes? "They killed Gypsies in Auschwitz and Treblinka and Buchenwald, and a half-dozen other camps. First, they tortured them and did terrible operations on them, and then they killed them."

"Not Gypsies!" Zoe denied it. She sat like stone.

How can she not believe me? Momma wondered. Who would make up such a terrible story? Who would play such a trick on a friend? On her best friend?

"In one concentration camp, Zoe, they say that the spirits warned a Gypsy prisoner, a thirteen-year-old boy, that on the next day all the Gypsies would die. He told the other prisoners and they staged such a riot that the Nazis couldn't stop them for many hours. But the spirits had told the truth. Next day all the prisoners were killed. All."

Zoe sat unmoving but no longer quarreling

with Momma's story.

"Aiye, the young boys, the young boys," Momma mourned. "They are our heroes. They die for us. What they suffer for us, Gypsy boys, Jewish boys, gentile boys—"

"Enough talk." Zoe broke in abruptly. "Now we must get to work for your son. Set the package with the clothes in the corner as far away from me as you can."

"Oh, can't I open it and show you the things in it? I even had the shoe salesman put in a tin of Griffin shoe polish and a buffing cloth because I know that in the army they teach how important it is to have shined shoes."

"Set it in the corner." Zoe watched Momma do as she was told. "The money." She extended her hand. "So it can be tested. Now kneel beside me, and you pray in your religion and I'll pray in mine." She held the money tight in her fist.

"Jews don't kneel," Momma said, with satisfaction. How wise of God to have made this rule. It was impossible for her to kneel. She would never be able to get up.

"Then I will go on my knees for you." And Zoe did, with a solid thump. "Close your eyes and pray."

Momma shut her eyes.

"Oh God, Oh Jesus, Oh Moses, help my friend," Zoe implored. Her pleas were loud and piteous.

"Bring Ben home. Bring her son back. *Bring him back home to his mother.* Bring him back to her!"

"*Oumain,*" Momma sang out. "*Oumain!*" Her thoughts were on him only now, on how he must look in this new King size that Zoe said he was. He had been a wiry adolescent and she had spent much time worrying about his eating. And now, a forty-two waist. Thank God! She tried to picture him plump, robust, but she could not.

"You can open your eyes," Zoe said. "The spirits have told me this money is cursed."

Momma clutched her blouse in fear.

"We must rid ourselves of this dirty money, and then I will be able to deliver a message from the spirits to you."

"But how did my money get cursed? Am I such a bad person?"

"No. You are a good woman. But somewhere sometime the money belonged to someone evil. A father who molested his daughter—"

Momma shuddered.

"—A son who killed his father." Zoe dangled the bills before her by thumb and forefinger. "It could be anything like that. The curse is on the money and it will stay there no matter what you do. Even if you change all your money for other money, the curse remains. There is only one way for you to get free of it; you must get rid of the money." She thrust the bills at Momma. "Tear them."

Momma ripped them once in half and then again and again. She tore without any feeling of regret. the way she might shred scrap paper. What was money compared to having Ben home? "What do we do next, Zoe?"

"You must flush these down the toilet. I will show you where." Momma followed her out back into a dark hall. A staircase rose there in the gloom, ghostly clothes and blankets swelling its banisters. "Up there," Zoe pointed.

"I can't see well," Momma apologized. "If I fall, my leg could get badly hurt and I want to be well for him when he comes. Would the spirits mind very much if you got rid of the money?"

Without a word, Zoe turned her around and led her back. "Close your eyes and wait here—and pray like you never prayed before." She waited until Momma was seated, eyes closed, and then she went back into the hall. Soon Momma heard the water rushing through the pipes and then again and again. Zoe was gone a long time.

Sitting alone in that dark draped sanctuary, Momma thought of that thirteen-year-old Gypsy boy who was martyred before manhood. Thirteen was a sacred age for a boy. Sorrowfully, she thought of Ben at thirteen. His bar mitzvah time. How she had worked, cleaning and cooking and baking. New beige curtains on the windows, and a new brown cretonne couch cover. Gefilte fish, stuffed cabbage, herring, sponge cake, egg-challah, honey-cake, whiskey, raisins and almonds, hard candy. An old fashioned bar mitzvah in the house. No *trayf* caterers with imitation chopped liver for her boy's coming of age. Even if she could have afforded it, she told herself and Sol many times, she would not have considered a catered bar mitzvah. How she had planned.

They would all come from the shul directly to the feast.

Who all? Who came?

Almost no one.

A few relatives who were too refined to eat much: the nibblers. Only Ike ate heartily, God bless him. The rabbi was there long enough for one glass of schnapps and he was gone. Three boys from Ben's bar mitzvah class stopped in, God bless them. They ate, giggling shyly, and they went.

Momma despaired. It was perfectly true that she did not mix with the neighbors, and she didn't make friends with every *yente* on the block, still on a bar mitzvah day she had believed that many well-wishers would come from the shul for a nosh and a good-luck drink. People were selfish; they had no time for anyone else.

Ben had tried to comfort her. "Don't mind, Momma. It's so delicious, I could eat it all."

And he had eaten with his friends and eaten again—but the day was spoiled. How much could a few boys—and Ike—together, how much could they eat?

"You have to invite people," her sister had said, "with printed invitations. If you want them to come, you have to invite them properly with RSVP's."

Lily was always criticizing. She thought because she was middle-class, she had the right.

"It's just too bad for them if they don't know enough to come by and wish a boy good luck. Poppa made the announcement in the shul," Momma answered her.

Lily was there with her prize of a husband, Irving (they parked the car two blocks away so that no one would see them driving on the Sabbath), and there Irving stood, picking his teeth with his pinkie nail. The two of them argued in the living room over the laden table while they nibbled gefilte fish daintily like it was caviar, quarreling over who should write the check for Ben, the check for twenty dollars.

"You do it. I spent plenty this month on the house."

"Why should I do it? What's he to me? He's *your* sister's son."

So they had separate checking accounts. So they were big shots. So what? On *Shabbos* who writes checks? Who gives money on *Shabbos*?

And Ben had accepted the check from Lily even though Momma said not to take it, not to touch money on the Sabbath. So badly did he want a full-size bike, he just couldn't turn the money away. Imagine, to fight like that just to show off the checking accounts. That memory was bile in Momma's throat.

"Finished," Zoe sang out as she let herself back into the *ofisa*. "Finished. Peace will come to you soon." She approached Momma. "Peace is on its way."

Momma looked at her hopefully.

"Dear friend, now I may give you the spirits' true message. While the water was flowing and washing away the dirt, the spirits reported that we had made a good start—but *all* your money is cursed. It brought you bad luck and it will kill your son if we don't work very fast."

"Help me, Princess Zoe. Please help me. Please."

Zoe narrowed her eyes. "Is your son's life worth five thousand dollars?

"What a question. A child's life! A child's life is worth any amount."

"The spirits knew you would feel that way. You are a true mother. Then you must move swiftly and get rid of the filthy five thousand dollars that lies in the bank destroying your family."

"But there are only four thousand dollars left—"

"True. Altogether it makes five. You have only the four thousand to worry about after this morning."

"I see."

"You must bring four thousand dollars next week. You must also bring one live healthy chicken with you. About three-and-a-half to four pounds."

"I would feel silly carrying a live chicken on the subway," Momma said apologetically. "I have to change trains and walk upstairs and downstairs and cross over—you know Canal Street. Besides, I think it must be against the law to carry a chicken on the subway." She could not remember ever having seen one. Probably they would figure it like a child under six and let it ride free.

"All right, all right. I will buy the chicken for you. But it must be *your* chicken. You must pay for it."

"Of course."

"Then it's all arranged. You will bring four thousand dollars in hundred dollar bills next week. That is your part. I will get the chicken for you."

"Zoe—" Momma followed her as she went through the curtains to the store door. "You are my best friend. I don't know what I'd do without you. When I first came to your door, I was ready to kill

myself. I was without hope. You gave me hope."
Gratitude choked her. She started out, head bowed,
and, turning once to wave good-bye to the Princess
standing in the doorway, she moved buoyantly down
the street.

TEN

In the morning and then again in the afternoon on Sunday, there was no minyan for prayers. Sunday was a bad day for the shul because it was visiting day on Long Island. All the *chaverim*—whose children and grandchildren had miraculously escaped from Williamsburg and migrated to the suburbs—this was their day to put on their best Klein's dresses or Ripley's suits, to fill their pockets with Charms and Life Savers and to hurry to Pennsylvania Station with their bundles and cake boxes. The minyan could more easily have been accomplished on the Atlantic Avenue Station.

The abbreviated afternoon prayer service was finished, but Sol still sat in the back of the empty, brightly-lit synagogue. Before him and up above in the women's balcony stretched row after row of red plush seats gaping open like mouths waiting to be filled. He remembered how Spitzer The Treasurer, Spitzer who came from Sol's own little village near Budapest, where they had read Rashi together forty years ago in *cheder*—how Spitzer had taken up a collection to buy the plush seats, how he had wheedled the money from the membership by joking and promising marvelous comforts if only they would give at least ten dollars apiece. That was the year before Ben's bar mitzvah, the year that the congregations had been so large that on Yom Kippur there wasn't standing room for all the mourners who came to the Yiskor service to remember their dead.

Yes, Ben had had his bar mitzvah with a good crowd watching him and wishing him success. A lot of good it did him. How beautiful he had been in his new talis and yarmulke, his firm young face flushed with excitement. How well he had done his *Haftorah*. Momma had put together three hundred brown paper bags of raisins and almonds and sweets; when the reading was completed, the women had rained down the bags from the balcony for the eager children waiting below to run for their sweets. There was so much noise, so much joy when the children ran that the shul rang with Jewish laughter. Spitzer was hit on the nose with one bag and he blamed his wife. She pleaded innocent; such a big nose, she said, who could miss it? They had laughed a lot in the shul that morning and the laughter had made him proud. Even though Momma wept in the afternoon when no one came to the house to share their bar mitzvah table— no one except the few relatives: high-class Lily and her big bargain, Irving, with the checkbooks—still, the morning in the shul shone like a bright jewel in Sol's memory.

He kept his small treasury of happy experiences carefully stored in his mind, and he reviewed them tenderly: how he had passed the American history test at naturalization and the judge had complimented him; how he had answered the boss who was trying to hurry him with a job he was doing—"What is this, a matzoh factory? I don't press matzohs. I press pants..."; how he had conquered Europe in Pershing's army so long ago; how he had enjoyed listening to his son at his bar mitzvah. All of these, the small golden nuggets in the tired empty bag of his life, he cherished. They were fragments of the goodness that life offered a man; the bits that were allotted to him, he was grateful for.

And now?

Now Spitzer the Treasurer was dead from high blood pressure and the bar mitzvah boy, *Alav Hasholam*, was dead from *hostilities*. The word was iodine in Sol's mouth. He looked down at his lap, at the two strong hands lying there, hands that spent the days pushing a great heavy gas iron over seams and wrinkles in custom-made pants. If only those hands could have smoothed life a little for Momma. If only for Ben.

The Almighty had not willed it.

Glancing once more at the Ark, he noted the brave golden lions guarding the tablet, and the red velvet curtains behind which lay the scrolls, and he was comforted. In God's house, at least, every man was a man.

Outside, the others were still kibitzing. There was the *shammes*, as always silent; Stein from the appetizing store, and Ike. Four Jews, counting himself, with time for prayers on a Sunday afternoon.

The *shammes* went in to turn off the lights and lock up.

"Sol—" Ike was worried about him.

Before prayers he had told Ike that the army's telegram had come; the funeral would be in four weeks. That was why Ike lingered here waiting. He was concerned.

—"Sol, you sat such a long time in there. How are you?"

"How is any Jew in a place where he can't find a minyan?"

"That's all that's bothering you? You should be used to it by now." Ike laughed raucously. "You should go to the Hasidim. They always have a minyan."

It was true. Since the end of World War Two, the neighborhood had become a Hasidic haven. As the prospering American Jews of the large synagogue moved away, a new population which worshipped in storefronts and tiny apartments took over. Even the vacant movie theater had become a Hasidic shul. The Hasidim despised the American Jews who, in turn, didn't care much for their mystical brethren.

"That *rebbe* down the street," Ike continued, "the Miracle Worker. He always has a minyan. That's his miracle."

"Let him have it and good health to him." Sol shrugged. "To his shul I don't go."

"You went one time—" Stein accused. He was a small man, emaciated and mean, his body sway-backed from years of scooping up herrings from barrels. "Once I saw you with the missus, and you were going into the *rebbe*'s storefront. Now don't tell me no. I saw you with my own eyes."

"Stein, an eagle should have your eyes, he wouldn't need eyeglasses. I went. I went with my wife all over: to the Miracle Worker; to Family Service, to the Red Cross, to Rabbi Zoffar. Our boy was missing and we tried to find some comfort, some peace...."

"So what did the Miracle Worker tell you? What?" Stein was hungry to know.

"Not much. He sat in his pure white clothing on a pure white bed filled with pure white feather pillows—and when he saw that I had no beard and my wife didn't wear a wig, he had no advice for us. He had no miracles for us. In fact, for us, he had nothing."

"And Rabbi Zoffar had for you something?" Stein was a scoffer. All his favorable opinions were based on profits he could expect for himself. From the rabbi he got only thoughts not tangible profits.

"What could Rabbi Zoffar have for me?" Sol responded.

He, who had been schooled in a European *cheder*, who had been lost in the New York shuffle, who had been destroyed in the national blood sport— Free Enterprise—he understood that if a rabbi offered a little comfort, that was all that one could ask. Try to explain to an insect like Stein that the rabbi's wisdom, his stories and parables each Sabbath, were rare gifts to be remembered and cherished all week.

How could Stein understand that in the shul a poor man had his one chance to be exalted. Stein only understood the exaltation of the deal.

"He told my wife to pray and to trust in the Almighty's wisdom," Sol said simply. "That was his advice."

"Such advice *any* man can give."

"I don't ask *any* man."

Ike interrupted them. "Look, isn't that the rabbi coming? See, crossing way down the block?"

"I have to work in the store," Stein said hastily, and off he scuttled.

"That's not the rabbi coming," Ike whispered,

as they watched the herring-dealer hurry away. "The rabbi can't walk so far so many times a day. I just said that to get rid of Stein."

"Why should he run from the rabbi?

"Ah, there's a story," Ike began with pleasure. "Yesterday in the afternoon—mind you, Saturday afternoon—Stein was walking his Nazi pedigree dog with the dragging belly and the frog legs. You know that brown freak? Such a dog belongs in a zoo, I tell him when he starts with how fancy the dog is. Papers, this dog has papers. I also have papers.

"Anyway, he was walking the dog in the Bridge Plaza Park and he saw the rabbi coming. Do you think Stein had enough shame to hide? No. He stayed right there. The rabbi came up to him and scolded him. 'Stein, it is forbidden to keep an animal tied up on the Sabbath.' And Stein, that no-goodnik, that lox-trimmer, answered him, 'Rabbi, this dog is my *kaddish*. You know I have no sons to pray for me after I am dead. Only this dog will be my *kaddish*.' This is Stein's idea of a big joke, to say such a thing to a rabbi. So the rabbi answered him, 'If this dog is your *kaddish*, then you have a better *kaddish* than your father had.'"

Sol began to smile. The smile became a chuckle and then bloomed into a hearty laugh as he enjoyed the joke. Rabbi Zoffar was a sage. It was a good thing to be alive to hear the stories of such a rabbi. Ike, watching his brother-in-law, enjoyed the joke anew with him.

"Who told you the story, Ike?"

"Who? Stein. Who else? He's so dumb he doesn't even know when to shut up."

Sol shook his head. It was astonishing that a man could be so stupid. Stein was wealthy: he owned his store and two apartment houses; he was always buying a new car. In America, Stein was a success. Momma was always talking about how an ignoramus like Stein was such a success.

Sol planned—he would postpone telling her the terrible news. It could wait. Tonight he would tell her the story of Stein and his dog. For the first time in so many months, he would give her something to smile about. To take her mind off her misery, for a minute.

ELEVEN

Sitting on the couch soaking her feet in a basin of warm water and epsom salts, Momma had the week's pile of newspapers beside her and she was systematically going through them reading the advertisements. She enjoyed bargains even if she didn't buy them.

"Where did you go this morning, Momma?" Sol asked.

"I had an errand."

"What kind of errand?"

"A private errand."

"So early on a Sunday?"

"Who are you, Mr. Keene, tracer of lost persons? Why are you giving me the third degree?"

"I'm just asking where you went so early on a Sunday."

"I know what you're asking. I had to go somewhere. *Nu*—"

Turning the page and spreading the newspaper out to its full width, she sent the message to him that she was busy with her reading.

Despair overtook him.

"Momma. The army sent me a telegram."

"So? They sent us plenty telegrams already. Too many telegrams. Western Union doesn't have to worry. Plenty telegrams."

"In four weeks, Momma, will be his funeral."

"Mmm, what a buy. May's has nylon curtains on sale tomorrow. Six ninety-eight a pair."

"You heard me, Momma? In four weeks will be Ben's funeral. He's here in America already on the west coast."

"I heard everything."

"I made arrangements with Park's Funeral Parlor on Eastern Parkway and with the shul. I would like our own rabbi for the funeral, but if you don't want Rabbi Zoffar, I'll look for someone else."

"Do what you please. Did you notice all the stores are having summer sales already? It's so early."

"They're sending soldiers with him, Momma. An honor guard. With guns. I know you wouldn't like the guns, but that's the army's way. They try to pay respects."

"They shouldn't fight in any more wars. That way they pay respects better. Look, here is Klein's advertising thousands of men's sport shirts at a dollar forty-nine nationally advertised at three ninety-five to four ninety-five. That's a buy, you have to admit."

Sol persisted. "The soldiers in the honor guard will all be Jewish boys. You wouldn't mind the honor guard?"

"Mind? I don't mind anything."

He knew he was in deep but he couldn't stop now.

"Momma?"

"I'm busy reading."

"Momma, what will we do with his clothes and his bicycle and his camera?"

Now she crashed the paper down and she was wild. "We'll do nothing. We won't touch a thing in that room, not one single thing, not even a scrap of paper. Do you hear me? Everything will stay right where it is."

"But some poor boy could use those things. What good are they lying here so long? The bicycle is rusty already."

"Everything will stay right as it is. They're not our things to touch. Promise me you won't go in there."

He shut his eyes.

"Promise!"

He had to tear the words out of his heart.

"I promise."

And still he didn't stop.

"And the insurance, Momma. I told you they

are sending us letters about his insurance."

Disgust contorted her face.

"No insurance. You want money from his blood? What kind of a father are you?"

"I am the father of a dead son."

Instantly she was sorry. If only she could tell him what she and Zoe knew—*Ben was not dead*! If only she could share the joys and the hopes of her heart with him. She wanted to so much.

The spirits would not allow it. She was not at liberty to do it yet.

Clumsily, she lifted her feet out of the basin of water and began to dry them.

"Sol, you want corn soup for supper? You like corn soup so I'll open a can of Lily of the Valley. I have it outside in the box in the hall. I'll warm it right away."

"Did you actually hear what I told you, Momma? Did you understand?"

"I understand everything. Corn soup will do. It has milk in it and you need a little milk. You don't get enough milk so tonight you'll have corn soup."

The farthest thing from his mind now was telling her about Stein and his dog. Her words had crushed the strength out of him, crushed his life, and the worst part of it was that she spoke them casually as if the insults were falling on a stone instead of on the head of a man. How was it that women used words like bullets? He was no philosopher. He didn't know any answers.

All he knew was that misery was a perpetual boarder in his house.

TWELVE

Sunday, June 3, 1951

 Pleased with herself, Momma smiled absently.

 Here she was on the train and the Dime Savings Bank said it was only seven-thirty. Sol had certainly been surprised when she rushed him through his breakfast. Too bad about him.

 It was true that she always urged him to eat slowly and digest calmly—but today she had an early appointment. She certainly wasn't going to tell him where or why.

 Maybe he thought she was going to another man?

 Plenty of women carried on that way.

 Let him think whatever crazy things he wanted to.

 He had done exactly what she asked him to. These days he questioned her less and less, leaving her pretty much alone. All she had to do was nod her head whenever he talked, nod and try not to smile so he wouldn't suspect a thing. Occasionally she caught him staring at her speculatively, but this didn't worry her. He was not to know what was going on—until the right time.

Her right time.

And Zoe's.

And Ben's.

Sol had lived with her for more than thirty years, yet he understood nothing about her. Good. That was why, this morning, he had quickly gulped his coffee without protest and was probably the earliest one in shul.

Her new corset pinched into her flesh in several places like paper clips. She longed for that first glimpse of the ferris wheel and the parachute jump; it would be like a view of the Promised Land.

When Stillwell Avenue came, it would not be a minute too soon.

These corsets were the first new ones in three years. Because now that she had to come out so often—now that she had so many business appointments—it was necessary to look presentable. She'd even treated herself to a store haircut, but that miserable barber on Lee Avenue—his sign said distinctly "Ladies and Gents Haircuts at $1.25"—he did such an awful job that she was sure she was his first lady customer in years. He had clipped her hair short, shaved her neck, and done no thinning at all. At that price! *Robber* should be on his sign: *Cutthroat,* not *Barber.* He had made her look years older.

Well, the hair was neat even if it wasn't fashionable.

And a bit of the natural black peeked through the gray. Momma crimped the back with her free hand.

Her other hand was tightly clasped around the large, new, brown pocketbook, imitation leather but so soft it felt real. She had bought it on Friday morning on her way to the bank.

Momma had never seen four thousand dollars at once, but she had the foresight to buy the large pocketbook to carry the money in.

The small everyday purse was certainly not sufficient. Not since she'd been single had she owned a large pocketbook. Her married finances had always been in coins and small bills.

Life was different these days.

She'd gotten a buy on the pocketbook because the gold clasp was slightly tarnished.

As if that made the slightest difference.

The clasp was hidden once the bag was tucked under her arm. And it was easy to press her thumb on the tarnished spot whenever she had to open it.

She stared down as Brooklyn receded and the Navy Yard lay spread out under the bridge. Her hand continued to grasp the pocketbook tightly, but the rest of her body relaxed, lulled by the rocking of the train.

Ben had been carried off over the water by a ship, a large ship nothing like the scruffy ones floating below. What a strange place the world was, a place in which an enormous vessel could just carry off her son to a remote land which meant nothing to her.

What should Korea mean to her?

She was no careful follower of the news. Headlines and first paragraphs were enough. Too much. Selected headlines in the *Daily News* and the *Post* and, of course, the *Journal American*.

Ever since she could remember, headlines screamed horror: starving slant-eyed children, famine, poison gas, strafing on Spanish roads, mutilated mothers, Jews and Jews and yet more Jews butchered like calves all over Europe, and after the Jews were finished off, atomic bombs and radiation, death and still more death.

International events no longer attracted her notice. The gossip columns were interesting: Cholly Knickerbocker and Walter Winchell wrote about people everyone knew who sometimes behaved scandalously and shocked her. She read recipes and advertisements of sales and apartment rentals and advice columns avidly.

So—suddenly there was a "police action" in

Korea.

What was a police action? And exactly where was Korea? Policing meant patrolling, keeping order. Order in a tiny country all cut up with mountains and valleys. Order meant control and supervision and direction. Order for the disorderly Orientals who did not have American know-how.

Order, not war.

Harry S—the "S" stood for nothing, actually, and as far as Momma was concerned he was good for nothing—Harry S Truman said it was not a war.

Remembering *The Good Earth* with Paul Muni and the incomparable Luise Rainier in it, Momma pictured Korea as a tiny China, quaint and poor. She had nothing against Asians. The world was big enough for all kinds. Live and let live.

Patrolling, after all, meant helping and supervising. Americans were bringing the modern age to people in a backward place.

Truman was not a man who loved war.

Truman was a haberdasher.

So how did it turn into fighting all at once?

Momma had missed something somewhere, and, afterward, she could never find out how it happened.

Poor Ben.

He found out.

He could just thank his lucky stars he had

Momma.

Because of her he would return to give her grandchildren, but she would never let him go away again, never let him take such a chance again. Just let Princess Zoe get him safely home and his army days would be over.

Momma would give him—if he so much as mentioned the army.

He belonged in school!

He was still young, just the right age for college.

He had finished high school in the army.

A dentist or even a doctor was possible.

She could taste the glorious words already: "My son Ben, the physician...."

Joy teemed through her body at the thought.

Delancey Street. The train jolted to a halt.

Momma smoothed her skirt over her knees and gripped the pocketbook firmly. Next was Bowery and then Canal Street, and there she had to change trains.

At the Bowery she rose and stood clinging to the slippery white pole, acutely aware of the fortune in her pocketbook. She looked about her, but no one else was in the car except an elderly conductor working the doors. Momma smiled at him acknowledging that they were both big-city people who knew the subways by heart.

Canal Street was next. How glad she would be to arrive in Coney Island, to get to Zoe and turn the money over. So much cash made her queasy.

When she'd handed the slip to the other teller—ducking her head low so Mr. Morse wouldn't see her—the busybody had rushed right over to Mr. Morse to show him the slip. And then Mr. Morse himself had come to the window to ask, "Are you closing out your account with us now, Mrs. Greenfield?"

"There are a few dollars left in the account, Mr. Morse," she'd had the presence to answer briskly.

Wasn't this America?

Wasn't it her own money?

Where did he get off with his cross-examination?

"Isn't it enough to keep an account open in your bank?"

"Certainly it's enough." Mr. Morse stood very close to the window and looked directly at her, his face troubled. "Mrs. Greenfield, are you angry with me for some reason?"

Momma was quite flustered.

This thin, long, refined face; this courteous, expressionless face that she had respected all the years was studying her anxiously from behind the slender bars of the teller's cage.

"No, Mr. Morse. Why should I be angry with

114

you? You've always been such a gentleman. This has nothing to do with you. After all the free calendars you gave me and all the fine service, how could I be angry with you? No. I just came to this window today for a change, a novelty."

He was still looking at her skeptically. "If I could have my money," she began urgently, "it's Friday and the kosher butcher will be very crowded. Of course, you wouldn't know about it, but Friday is a very busy day in a Jewish home...."

The train was pulling into Stillwell Avenue when Momma made her resolution. *If* the spirits said this money was clean, she would take it right straight back to Mr. Morse. She would take all future deposits to him too. If he cared that much—if he was a little sweet on her—he was a nice man and deserved her patronage.

Scooting off the train, she then paused to look at herself in the mirror of the Wrigley gum machine on the open platform. Daylight revealed too much. She was always dismayed by her image in the sunlight—and by snapshots that bossy relatives insisted on taking.

Surely her face was not so sunken-in and pouched just because some of her teeth were missing.

Surely her neck was not so corded and chicken-skinned.

What made her face powder turn into white

floury dust through which age cracked?

What had happened, Momma wondered, in despair; what had happened to the plump, comely, black-haired girl; to the handsome young woman who had once been pursued by an accountant? Time had devoured her.

Blinking back sudden tears, Momma hurried along the wooden planking.

Careful, she cautioned herself. No missteps, no tumbling now.

A life is in the balance.

THIRTEEN

Momma, seeing Zoe in the doorway with her hand shading her eyes, waiting, quickened her pace happily.

So her friend was anxious for these visits too.

Friendship was more precious than gold.

Zoe came forward several steps to meet her. "I'm ready, my dear," she said softly. "I searched the whole building today to be sure it's empty so there will be no human witness. What we do is not meant for other eyes."

Momma trembled.

Zoe led her in, this time past the *ofisa*, through the curtains, into a private little back room, the walls of which were completely draped with heavy curtains and rugs.

These dusty thick hangings insulated the room in perpetual darkness, and Zoe did not turn on any light. The draperies, the musty air heavy with the odor of old incense, the deep silence of the deserted building all closed in on Momma making her feel as if she had entered some long-sealed tomb.

Backing up against the curtained wall, she kept her eyes on Zoe, suddenly apprehensive.

Her foot pressed down on some object. Bravely forcing herself to look down, she saw an abundance of litter on the floor: bottles, cigarette butts and other small garbage. A twisted crust had caught onto her sole and it clung there like a snake. She scraped her foot back and forth trying to work it off the shoe.

"My dear, I was about to sweep when you came," Zoe said hastily. "I must cleanse this room and get it ready with *you* in it. *You* must be here while I purify it. Gypsies really belong to the outdoors, in tents with the earth for our floor. I made this room my tent—" she pointed to the draped walls—"and this floor my open field. Now it must all be purified."

For the first time since she'd met Zoe, Momma felt uncertainty.

The store windows were so clean.

Zoe was so personally elegant.

How could a Princess live on such a floor?

For one wild moment, Momma knew panic and was tempted to flee.

But where?

To what refuge?

She squelched her doubts. Zoe was right, of course. Momma remembered from her childhood the music teacher with the pitch pipe and the song she had taught them:

> Tonight you'll sleep in a cold open field,
> Along with the raggle taggle Gypsies, O....

The fields, the wide open fields, that was where they truly belonged. Not behind stores but out in the open.

Nature's people. Simple and free.

Zoe was working with a soft broom, hurriedly brushing together the litter on the floor.

"We are wanderers on the earth," she said to Momma.

"Yes, I know. Nature's own children. I was just thinking that."

"You are right." Zoe moved the broom in short quick strokes.

Momma's eyes stayed focused on the floor.

"You know why we became wanderers?" Zoe asked, as she pushed the rubbish toward the center. "You know why Gypsies wander—and why sometimes they steal small things?"

Momma looked up, startled. To have a Gypsy Princess admit that some Gypsies steal was remarkable.

Princess Zoe must be very fond of her indeed, Momma decided, to speak to her so frankly. It was embarrassing. Momma was unused to confidences.

"No. Why do they steal?"

"When the Je—when they started to crucify Christ—"

"The Jews did not crucify him. The Romans did," Momma corrected tartly.

Did this Gypsy Princess with the floor for her open field think that she was dealing with an ignoramus?

Why, the church itself admitted that the Jews were falsely blamed. She had read in the *Journal American* where priests said so. Not that she needed *them* to tell *her*.

"Of course it was the Romans. The priests told me wrong when I was a kid, but I never believed them," Zoe soothed. "When the *Romans* were about to crucify Christ, a Gypsy tried to steal away the nails. There were four nails, two for His hands, one for His feet, and one very long spike for His heart. The Gypsy managed to steal the spike.

"The soldiers tried to find it, but they couldn't find it anywhere. They suspected the Gypsy and began to beat him but he wouldn't tell. So Jesus looked down from His Cross and told the Gypsy that from then on his people could wander over the earth taking what they need. And Gypsies live that way. They help others like that Gypsy helped Christ—or like I help you. They do good. But sometimes they need a little money or food so they take it. Can you blame them?"

"Mmmmm." Momma didn't care to answer that one directly.

She thought that Jesus was a trifle high-handed but she kept from saying so.

None of this story involved Jews so it was not her business.

It was just not her religion.

Zoe had brushed the refuse onto a shirt cardboard. Now she disposed of it and the broom in the hallway, quickly.

"Now it's clean in here the way the good Lord meant it to be," she noted contentedly and crossed herself.

Momma approved.

Whoever said Gypsies were pagans? Every other word out of Zoe's mouth was God. They were really pious people. One wouldn't expect a pagan to know that cleanliness was next to godliness.

"Zoe, don't you worry about roaches with the dirt on the floor? I mean, it's not really a field...."

"I have a special Gypsy recipe I use and it gets rid of everything: rats, roaches, bats and evil spirits. Everything bad."

"Would it be asking too much for you to give me the recipe?" Momma asked it timidly.

"Well, it is a Gypsy secret...." Zoe weighed the question in silence. "But if you promise never to tell anyone else, then—when we have finished with your son's safety—I'll tell you. But you must promise."

"Of course."

"You have the money with you, dear?"

Holding forth the new purse like a tray, Momma expected her to notice and admire it.

"Take the money out."

Momma pressed the clasp—in this dim room it didn't look tarnished at all—and she took out the thick packet of bills banded together by a sturdy rubber band.

Zoe accepted the money without a word, snapping the rubber band onto her braceleted wrist. Wetting her forefinger, she counted.

"If you wouldn't mind," Momma said hesitantly, "I wonder if I might have the rubber band back. It's the one I use to keep my recipes together. You know, recipes that I clip out of the newspapers."

"Of course you must have it back, dear." Zoe handed it over immediately. "I'm glad you thought of it because nothing but the money must be tested for evil. But if I were you, I'd get rid of that handbag. It's been soiled by the money. Just toss it on the floor far away from us and I'll sweep it out later."

Obediently, Momma removed from the new pocketbook her small purse, her handkerchief, and the retrieved rubber band. She was sorry to see the pocketbook go; it had been such a marvelous bargain.

But thinking of what was about to be accomplished here this morning, she was immediately happy, gay, quite lightheaded. She was almost— almost young.

"Nothing but the money must be tested," Zoe repeated, as she took a large paper shopping bag from the great trunk. She slid Momma's money into the bag and flattened the bills on the bottom. Then she busied herself lighting three incense sticks which she arranged in an ashtray on the floor near Momma. From the *ofisa* she brought the glowing, rosy, votive candle in its glass, and, after murmuring a long prayer in which Jesus, Mary, and someone named Saint Sarah figured prominently, she crossed herself and meditated.

"Now I will get your chicken," she said at last. "But first you must pay me two dollars and thirteen cents so that when I bring it into this room, it will be *your* chicken."

"Two dollars and thirteen cents is high for a chicken," Momma observed mildly.

"For a beautiful, healthy, five-pound chicken?"

"Oh no," Momma conceded, "for a five-pounder it's a bargain."

She counted out the money, all the while congratulating herself that she had entrusted Zoe to do the buying. If she, herself, had bought this one in the kosher store, It would have cost far more.

Her finger on her lips, Zoe tiptoed through the curtains.

The spirits were about to descend, Momma could tell. She could sense a subtle change in the room, a heaviness of the air, an increasing warmth. Her face was moist with sweat and her dress clung to her back, soaked.

In came Zoe with a white hen, its feet tied together.

"Look, see how healthy it is," Zoe whispered, lifting a wing and blowing the feathers apart.

It *was* a healthy hen, but, poor Zoe, if she thought this was a five-pound fowl she was sadly mistaken. At Gypsy matters she was an expert, but in the chicken market, Momma could see, she needed help.

Perhaps, Momma planned, one day when she had a little time, she could show Zoe what to look for in a good soup chicken or a plump little pullet.

Thrusting the chicken into the bag on top of the money. Zoe held the bag tightly closed and began to pray Gypsy prayers and to rock back and forth on her gold high-heels. She moaned and she sobbed and she prayed; no spirits could fail to heed *her*.

Momma scrunched her eyes shut and whispered a brief prayer of her own to the One and Only God, her body pulsating with hope.

Please God. Please. Send Ben home. It's not much to ask, really. Just send him home. Don't let him kill anyone, and don't let him be hurt—such a sweet boy—but send him back the way he went, innocent of blood.

The chicken gave one ear-piercing shriek.

"Oh God!" Momma screamed. "Please, God!"

Zoe stiffened and for one frightful minute she was rigid, her eyes rolling until only the whites showed. Saliva dribbled out of her mouth and down her chin.

"Jesus—Mary—Joseph—and Sarah!" she gasped.

She opened the bag and turned it upside down. Out onto the newly swept floor tumbled the limp, white, feathered body.

"Dead!" Zoe exulted. "Dead just like I thought! Your money is cursed. It killed your chicken. But thank God your son is still alive."

"He isn't dead." She embraced Momma roughly. "He's going to live!"

"Oh, Zoe, how can I thank you?" Momma felt weightless; she too was a spirit, floating, set free.

"Don't thank me. You are my friend." Zoe turned her gaze to the chicken, glowering at it. Then she poked it with her toe.

"You know," she began, "a chicken has no soul, so I can't transfer the evil to it. There is only one way for us now. The money must be burned."

"If it must," Momma said shakily, "but those are our life savings."

"Oh? I asked you once if your son's life had a price." Zoe's words were scathing. She stood face-to-face with Momma, her hands on her hips, the slack paper shopping bag hanging from her right wrist. "Here. Take the dirty money back."

She thrust the bag at Momma.

"No!" Momma covered her eyes. "Burn it. Burn it all."

There was an unbearable silence. Zoe didn't move and Momma was terrified that she had spoiled everything. Zoe was such a good friend, and she, Momma, had not been worthy.

Then—thank God—Zoe relented and forgave her.

With her foot, Zoe shoved the dead chicken to the side of the room near where the polluted pocketbook lay. From her hallway, she dragged in a new tin garbage can which she set in the center of the room.

She wrapped the excess paper of the shopping bag round and round the money, and then she reached way down into the can and maneuvered her hand around until she'd located exactly the right spot to place the packet.

Momma, watching these preparations, was relieved that from where she sat she could not see what was being done.

Best not to know such things.

From the trunk, Zoe brought supplies: a small vial and a handful of sacred crystals. She sprinkled the crystals first and then poured a liquid into the can.

"Lighter fluid," she explained to Momma, "to see that every filthy scrap is burned."

Quickly, she struck a match and bent over the can with it.

Billows of white smoke began to puff over the rim almost at once.

Momma, watching, had the strangest sensation that there was ammonia pouring into the room.

She held her nose.

Perhaps the spirits were driving out the evil, cleansing all with this strong disinfectant. With so much magic around, unexpected things were bound to happen.

Still more smoke arose.

How pretty, Momma thought, her eyes smarting. How marvelous. Like Aladdin's lamp.

In those billows of smoke, Momma had a vision of Ben, of her hopes, pure and clear, rising from behind the bloody curtain of war. She would have him back soon.

What could stop him now?

How beautiful he had been as an infant, his skin as soft as a powder puff and his hair feathery light and curly. And he had been so clean! What other little boy cried whenever he got his hands soiled? Why, she'd never even allowed him a toy gun.

Weapons upset her. She believed that the way you train the child so he grows.

Now officious ignoramuses were trying to tell her that *this* boy was dead in a war.

A boy who never even owned a bean shooter. When the smoke began to thin, Zoe came to her to raise her up.

Looking deep into Momma's eyes, she crooned, "Now only good will come to you. Your son will return strong and well. You have loved him and helped him. God will be good to you."

She thrust her face closer to Momma's. "Do you believe?"

"I believe. Oh, of course, I believe, Zoe."

Momma stanched the sudden flow of tears with the back of her hand. "With all my heart, I believe. I don't mean to nag you, but things are hard at home. The army says he's really dead. There will be a funeral...." Her voice broke. "They send so many letters and telegrams. Now they are saying there is ten thousand dollars insurance money because he is dead. My husband says we must answer. It's so hard, Zoe. So hard."

"I know. I know all," Zoe soothed. "You must not take any money. You must wait for the spirits to guide you."

"Of course I won't take any money. Even if he were dead, I wouldn't want blood money."

"You must wait for the spirits to guide you," Zoe stressed.

"I will wait. You know I will. But I pray that the spirits will hurry themselves up a little."

"And I'll pray with you."

Zoe sank down on her knees and covered her face with her hands, staying that way for a very long time.

When she finally rose, she was severe with Momma.

"Now you may not come back here until I send for you. Wait at home. I must have time alone with the spirits. I will let you know when your son sails. Come in the front of the store and write your name and address on a piece of paper for me. I will notify you the minute I can."

She led Momma out slowly.

Momma found herself so weak she could barely shuffle along, and her eyes, unaccustomed to the light, stung.

In the store, Zoe handed her a pencil stub and a slip of paper, and Momma wrote out the address as clearly as she could.

Watching Zoe carefully fold that paper and then tuck it in her bosom, Momma was overcome.

"Thank you for helping me," she murmured, and impulsively took Zoe's hand and would have kissed it.

Zoe freed herself.

"I help you because you are my sister. Our people are like one people."

She pinched the tongue of the bell, silencing it as she opened the door.

Momma didn't move.

"Ah, there's my husband," Zoe noted in surprise. "See him sitting in that black car down the street? You never met him did you?" She smiled warmly. "He's dying to meet you. I've told him what a good friend I have."

"Have you really told him about me?"

"Only what a good mother you are. What a good woman. Maybe he would give you a ride home. Come."

"Zoe, that's such a beautiful car."

"A Gypsy man has to have the best and live the best. That's how it is. Men are like that."

Didn't Momma know that?

Didn't she always give Sol the bigger and better portions of food?

Didn't he get a new suit every Passover because he went to business? She stayed at home, so what did it matter if she wore old cotton house dresses to cook and clean in?

Still, Momma stood fast.

She sensed that Zoe was ready to say good-bye, and she wanted to postpone that as long as possible.

"Zoe, all my life I had to struggle with roaches. If you could tell me what to do, I'd be so grateful."

"Take some red pepper in an old plate—a sardine can is good—then light up the pepper with a wooden match. Be sure all the windows are closed up to keep the smell in the house. A strong stink will rise from the burning pepper and fill all the rooms. It won't hurt you, and it will drive away everything bad: rats, roaches, bats, ghosts, bad luck. It will chase them all."

"How remarkable."

"It really is. And you just watch that plate while the pepper is burning hot. Sometimes the powder seems to glow—and you see the face of a beloved one."

"Zoe!"

"I'm not promising. Not everyone sees it. If you're lucky, you will. A clean house is nice for a boy to come to."

"I'll do it tonight."

Taking her under the arm, Zoe propelled her along toward the car.

The husband must have seen them coming because he got out of the car and stood alongside it waiting.

Momma scrutinized him with the greatest interest.

He was tall and robust, handsome, with thick shining hair. Quite the right husband for a princess.

"You are Zoe's friend so you must be my friend." He inclined his head and body slightly.

"How do you do, Mr.—"

"Rollo," he said.

"How do you do, Mr. Rollo."

"Just Rollo. No Mister. Plain Rollo."

Momma could have sunk through the sidewalk at her own stupidity.

Zoe spoke up urgently.

"Rollo, I must do something for my friend right away in the *ofisa*. She is tired. Will you give her a ride home?"

"Oh, I couldn't—" Momma protested.

"Sure," Rollo said, opening the car door. "My pleasure."

"Remember, you must not come back till I send word," Zoe murmured. "You must let me communicate with the spirits in peace."

"Oh Zoe, I'll miss these visits. I feel like—like Eddie Cantor. You know. 'I love to spend each Sunday with you. As friend to friend, I'm sorry it's through—'" Her voice quavered.

Clasping her hand firmly, Zoe maneuvered

her into the car. "Good-bye," she said. "Good-bye, my friend."

She turned away and was gone without looking back.

FOURTEEN

"This is a very handsome car. Very classy. What make is it—Oldsmobile?" Momma chatted nervously.

Lily bought a new Oldsmobile every two years and always talked car, car, car. Her every sentence, even if it was to excuse herself to go to the bathroom, had an Oldsmobile in it. This car was as nice as any of Lily's cars.

Nicer, maybe, even though the thought was disloyal.

He went round to his side and opened the door and smiled down at her. "No. It's no Oldsmobile. It's a Cadillac convertible."

Momma was dazzled.

Family loyalty dissolved in the intensity of his charm.

"It's the best looking car I've ever seen."

"Thank you, Madame. Thank you." He got in and settled himself comfortably beside her.

"Just drop me at the station on Stillwell Avenue," Momma suggested. " That would be a great help."

"No. Zoe said 'Take my friend home,' so I take you home. I don't think you closed your door good. Open it and close it again."

Momma grabbed hold of the door handle, and, swinging the door open wide, she slammed it.

"Lady—it's a new car. You don't slam a new car door like that. You could break it."

"Sorry. I thought that's the way to be sure it's really closed."

"Not this car. See—" He reached across her lap and opened the door again, and then he swung it shut easily. "Like this. Maybe in an Olds or some other cheap car you got to bang the doors but never in a Caddy."

"I see," Momma said meekly.

She only wished Lily could hear him calling her car cheap. Gypsies were bold. They said whatever they thought.

He started the car.

Momma sat mute. She was so sorry she had slammed the door. The few cars she had ever ridden in had doors that only closed that way.

What did she know about fancy new cars?

Edging herself into the center of her seat, she made sure she wasn't leaning on the door. He had closed it so gently, who knew if it was actually locked?

"You like my car?" he asked as he glided it to a stop at a red light. Not like her brother-in-law, Irving, who drove like a bump-a-car ride in Coney Island.

"It's wonderful. It's like an airplane."

An airplane—or, for that matter, this open convertible—was as foreign to her as a space ship. Suddenly she was concerned about catching cold with all that wind blowing on her head and throat.

But it was a gentle friendly wind on a glorious summer day.

And Ben would be home soon!

Rollo clicked on the radio twirling dials until he got a Spanish singer accompanied by castanets and deafening brassy music.

Exotic, Momma thought   Probably WEVD. Sunday mornings they tried to please every group with a mish-mash of programs. She always tuned in to the Yiddish hour.

But it wasn't WEVD. Because once the Spanish song was over the announcer said he was going to play an oldy. Sure enough, there was the voice of Frances Langford:

"Red sails in the sunset, way out on the sea,
Oh carry my loved one home safely to me...."

"Lovely," Momma sighed.

Rollo hummed.

The drive home was swift, smooth, and unreal—a dream.

Once they turned onto Roebling Street in Williamsburg, he slowed down.

"Your house must be near. Right?"

She nodded.

"I'll drop you off here. It's easier for me to get back from here."

It was an excellent idea.

What if Sol or that *yente*, Mrs. Stein, or some other busybody saw her getting out of this fine car? What if they saw her with such a handsome, dark-skinned stranger? All she needed was that kind of scandal at her age.

"Leave me on this corner right in front of Western Union, please."

"Good-bye, Madame."

"Thank you for the lovely ride."

"It was a pleasure." He smiled most winningly as she left the car.

This was courtesy such as Momma hadn't experienced in years. She had thought such behavior was dead. She was thrilled.

Forgetting herself—in the heady power of his amiability—with all her might she slammed the car door.

FIFTEEN

"I would ask you to come up a minute, Ike, but Momma probably isn't home."

"So where is she?"

"To tell the truth, I don't know. Sunday mornings she goes out early and she stays away till late. When she comes home, she soaks her feet and rests like she walked the whole city. A few times she mentioned Coney Island—"

"Coney Island? You must be wrong."

"No. I see her emptying sand out of her shoes. Last Sunday she brought me a big clam shell to use for an ashtray. She said she found it."

"But she hates Coney Island. Even when we were kids she didn't like it. And you're telling me that now—with her arthritis—*now* she goes to walk in Coney Island?"

"You know your sister." Sol shook his head helplessly. "The tea-leaf readers are in Coney Island."

"Who? You mean fortune tellers? You let her

go to those crooks?"

"What can I do, lock her up? You know that orthodox Jews dasn't believe in such trash. In the sacred books it's written that fortune-tellers and wizards are abominations of God. In the proper time, people get to know what God wills. But your sister is superstitious. She believes everything: newspaper horoscopes, lucky numbers, tea leaves, bumps on the head. Everything."

"But that's crazy," Ike protested. "She knows better."

"I argue with her. I tell her it's true that some mystic rabbis believed that stars affected nations. But even *they* felt that Jews were above such influences. *Nu*—try to tell Momma. Her answer is all the big Hollywood stars believe in horoscopes. I tell her Hitler was also big with the astrology, but what does she care what I say?"

"Sol—" Ike was very agitated— "if she's going to Gypsies, you'd better put a stop to it. I'm afraid for her. A few times these past weeks, I saw her smiling to herself at jokes inside her head. Something is not right."

"You think I don't try to stop her? To find out? She can't listen to anything I say. She's too miserable. Your mother taught her to believe *Rahmanim bene rahmanim*. Jews must be against violence and killing. Merciful descendants of merciful ancestors. This is what she repeats.

"After Ben went to the army, she couldn't sleep. She would walk around the whole night thinking about the war. She's crazy on the subject, you know that, Ike?

"Every chance she gets now, she blames me because I was once a soldier. Because I served in the First World War and I walked my feet off and I lay in the trenches with mud and lice. Everything is my fault."

"Sol, don't listen to her."

"My feet were frostbitten. My nerves were shot from the shells. Still, I came home. I was lucky.

"For that, she *blames* me. Ike, tell me, how is it my fault that I came back and he didn't?"

"She doesn't know what she is saying."

"She begrudges that I was in Paris and I talk about it. You know what she says, night and day?

"That I made war glamorous for him and that's why he enlisted. Because I told him the story of how when I was in Paris, and I was walking on the big avenue with the trees, I noticed a young lady in front of me was losing her bloomers.

"I was a young buck in those days, so I went right up to her and said, 'Excuse me, Mademoiselle, but you are losing your bloomers.'

"And she kissed me on the cheek, right here near my ear, and then she stepped out of those bloomers like a regular drum major and strutted off leaving them behind.

"My buddies razzed me. 'Take 'em for a souvenir, Greenfield. Greenfield takes Paris by the bloomers.'

"What harm did I mean by that story, Ike? It happened."

Ike had heard the story many many times before and he always enjoyed it.

"No harm, Sol. No harm. Don't feel bad about it. About your Paris story you shouldn't worry. But about the Gypsies, you better worry. I mean it, Sol. You have to watch her."

"I'll watch. I'll watch everything. What else have I got to do?" He put his hand on his brother-in-law's shoulder. "I'm going upstairs now, Ike. *Shalom.*"

Wearily, he climbed the stoop steps and then entered the dark hall and began to go up. Twice today he'd made the walk to the almost deserted shul. If this kept up there would be no more shul. Long Island would be the haven for all the Jews that Hitler didn't get.

An overpowering stench filled the hall, a burning rancidity that caused him to gag. It wasn't the singeing odor of chicken feathers, nor was it the sweet charred scent of burned cake. It was acrid, strong, and unfamiliar, and it increased as he came higher up the stairs toward his own apartment.

He opened the door.

Momma, holding her nose with a handkerchief, stood by the closed window staring down into a sardine tin on the window sill. Whatever was in that tin was sending out the noxious fumes.

A dreadful idea came to him: poisoned air. He remembered the gas from the War. She was committing suicide!

"Shut the door," she snapped.

Did she want him to join her?

He covered his nose with his handkerchief. The odor was unbearable.

Momma was in a frenzy. Just now he had to come home?

Just now?

She had done everything exactly right: set out the pepper in the sardine tin, sealed up all the windows tightly, lit the pepper properly. Everything had been perfect and just now—when the pepper was charred, when it was time to watch for the wonderful magical vision—just now, her lousy luck, he had to come home and spoil it.

"I'm busy," she said, keeping her eyes fixed on the sardine tin, blocking it with her body so that if the dear face of her beloved son should appear, Sol would not be frightened.

"I see how busy you are. I'm going to open a

window."

"Don't you dare! Don't you dare do it!" she screamed.

"Tell me what's going on in my house or I'll open all the windows. Every window and the door too. Right now." He went into the kitchenette and began to work the lock on the window there.

"I'm getting rid of the roaches, the ants, and the mice. Now you know. Don't touch that window. Don't you dare. Do you do the housework? Are you the *cleaniker*? Do the roaches bother you? And the mice and the beetles? No, I'm the one who has to struggle with them. So now I have a formula to exterminate them and you want to spoil it. Big shot—"

She began to cough, great retching coughs.

Sol, realizing that she had been inhaling the poisonous fumes much longer than he, quickly pushed open the window. Then he moved as fast as he could, opening the others.

She coughed harshly, choking for air.

Quickly, he brought her a wet washcloth and a glass of water.

"Drink," he ordered, "and put the washcloth over your face."

The coughing paroxysms were so bad she was doubled over. She had to obey.

"Who gave you the powder?" he demanded of

her buried face. "A murderer?"

"A friend. A friend gave it to me." Arching her neck defiantly, she kept her face swathed in the washcloth. "You don't know her."

"In the old country we had a saying," Sol told her bitterly, 'If you have such a person for a friend, you don't need an enemy.'"

Lifting the washcloth off her mouth so it was a tent on her face, she raged. "You know plenty wise sayings, but you didn't know enough to keep *him* out of the Boy Scouts. You signed for him to first wear a uniform. You with all your stories of the war and what a hero you were with the frostbite and the Paris with the bloomers."

She snatched the cloth from her face.

"You taught him how to be a hero all right. Tell me a wise saying for what happened to him. Tell me. Talk!"

"I have nothing to tell you. Except it is a pity that in your heart you can't remember that he was my son too."

SIXTEEN

Sunday, July 1, 1951

There was the air of a matinee about Park's black and white marquee on Eastern Parkway with the crowd assembling beneath it. The glass-enclosed black schedule board was programmed "GREENFIELD 11:00 A.M." in white plastic clip-on letters.

Two identical, heavy, young women with wedding cake hair-dos, tiered and swirled, teetered on their high heels as they consulted the day's program.

"Boy, the Greenfields are lucky. They got the whole funeral home to themselves today. Sometimes you come here there are four-five funerals at a time, a regular factory."

"You're so right. Even now I could hardly believe it. Ben was such a nice boy, such a lively kid. Let's go get a cuppa coffee. A person needs something a time like this."

Near the curb, the black-visored funeral chauffeurs lounged and smoked eyeing the arrivals diffidently.

Relatives seized one another, embraced and wondered loudly why it was they only met at funerals, then lowered their voices and wept.

Lieb, the undertaker, a dapper little man with a pencil-thin mustache and black pointy shoes, his navy blue suit made piquant by the fresh pink rosebud in his lapel, moved discreetly among the crowd.

"Greenfield Services will commence shortly," he murmured to people. "Greenfield Services? Are you here to pay your last respects to Private Greenfield? Services will commence shortly."

Sol, seeing the undertaker circulating about the lobby, stayed as far away from him as possible. His interview with Lieb when he had come to make the arrangements for this funeral had been a horror.

Park's Funeral Home had a contract with the shul, and though the establishment was under new management the contract was permanent. So here Sol had come with simple requests.

No embalming.

No viewing, of course.

No music.

No flowers.

A plain pine box.

Lieb, on hearing the last specification, had

interrupted Sol to inquire softly, "Is this the kind of send-off you want to give your only son?"

To which Sol could only scream, "Send-off? *Send-off*? What kind of talk is that?"

"I only meant we have very fine Cedar of Lebanon—from Israel," Lieb explained hastily. "A very special box for a very special person."

Sol could not believe his ears.

"What are you, a candy salesman with the fancy boxes? I'm burying my only son and you're talking fancy with the boxes!" Sol could not contain his rage. "The Talmud says a plain wooden box for rich and poor alike, so how dare you start peddling fancy caskets? How dare you have here metal, and quilting, and imported wood? For Jews? Apostate! *Apikoiros*! A Jew you can't be."

"Nobody follows those old-fashioned rules any more, Mr. Greenfield," the undertaker had tried to defend himself. "These days mostly people are using silver caskets."

"Silver? Who uses silver? They bury gangsters in silver caskets, not Jewish boys. To the Mafia give silver caskets, not to Ben Greenfield."

Biting his lip, Sol had glared at Lieb, and he could see that the man was frightened.

"You will give me a plain pine box for my boy and you will obey the orthodox rules or I will go to the secretary and I will tell him no more business from the shul for Lieb; Lieb is a number one *Apikoiros*."

"Everything will be just as you wish, Mr. Greenfield. I just thought it was my professional duty to inform you of the latest trends."

"You thought wrong. Remember what I tell you. No music. No flowers. No fancy ceremonies. I want a Jewish funeral. Rabbi Zoffar, himself, will conduct the service. No trimmings."

"Just as you please."

"Not as *I* please. As the Talmud commands. You heard maybe of the *Talmud*?"

Lieb had no answer for that.

SEVENTEEN

Various helpful neon signs and directional arrows flickered in the undertaker's carpeted lobby accenting the theatrical decor.

Sol pushed through the leatherette swinging doors of the CHAPEL after leaving Momma in the INTIMATE FAMILY WAITING ROOM.

The chapel was quiet and too warm though huge gilt fans whirred high above like the wings of angels. The grass-green carpet lay spotless and lint-free, and the whole dim chamber had the air of being newly vacuumed for company. Tall, slender basket-urns of plastic white lilies stood along the center aisle marking the first dozen rows.

On a low catafalque at the front of the long room lay the rectangular flag-draped box, a diminutive base under the lavish flag, looking incongruously like a coffee table buried under a rich bright banquet cloth.

Four young sentries guarded it.

Two stood, feet apart, hands resting on their

rifles in front of them. The other two, their guns propped against the coffin, were drinking coffee from containers and eating jelly doughnuts.

Startled by the swishing sound of the doors, the doughnut eaters looked for a place to hide their pastries from Sol who walked slowly down the aisle toward them.

His eyes were fixed on the box so small under the great flag.

"Sorry, Sir. We thought there wouldn't be no harm in us having sinkers and coffee. We been here guarding all night."

"From who are you guarding him? From crooks?"

"Orders, Sir. Government orders."

"The government is very thoughtful."

The four of them stared at him.

He understood what was going through their heads: *The father. That's when this funeral duty gets rough, when the family comes around.*

The soldier turned away from Sol and covered his mouth to silence a belch. Respect was necessary.

"I could do without such government thoughtfulness."

The soldier who had offered the explanation flinched at those words making Sol sorry he had spoken them. This soldier looked to be about nineteen, skinny, with a long sallow face, like a sweet potato, tapering away to no chin. A dull-looking, quiet boy.

Still, he was alive for all his dull looks, and inside the coffin were the remains of Sol's lively handsome Ben.

"My son died a long time ago," Sol said gently. "Drink your coffee. Eat your doughnuts."

The army knew what it was doing.

Ben belonged with these boys because he had been an average American boy. He, too, would eat sinkers with his coffee—at home, Momma had only let him drink milk—and he would have belonged with them just because he was an ordinary American.

He had shed his Judaism after his bar mitzvah faster than a snake sheds its skin. How he had wanted to be one hundred percent American!

Momma could fool herself, but Sol knew in his heart that Ben had been just an ordinary boy. No scholar; no genius or world-beater, but a nice person. A good son. Now the earth would cover him up and no one but his parents would notice that he was gone, that there was a void in the world.

In his short life there had been the sweet promise that he would one day be a man—with luck, a good man—and that promise was broken, for he was dead. Simple. Dead is dead.

The soldiers did not go on eating and drinking. Sol could see that he had upset them. Before he came in, it had been just a box to them that they freighted across the country, just a box with some poor Joe in it who had put up his head at the wrong time in the rice paddies.

Now, Sol understood, his presence had turned that anonymous poor Joe into a person, a person like themselves. They looked really uncomfortable.

"Since there's no viewing," the soldier spoke up again, nervously, "we thought it would be okay to take a break. After all, the funeral doesn't begin till eleven."

"My son wouldn't mind," Sol soothed him, "and I don't mind. In fact, if you could spare a sip of that coffee—"

Both containers were instantly thrust at him.

There was nothing he wanted less at the moment. But he took first one and then the other.

He had to struggle to keep from gagging.

"*L'chaim*," he said softly, and he drank from each.

EIGHTEEN

Momma sat in the waiting room on a mahogany armchair.

Sitting this way, alone, she was reminded of her wedding when she had been seated on just such a chair by her father and she had remained there, secluded, until the ceremony.

An orthodox bride never mingles with the guests; she just sits quietly apart and the women come in to admire her veil and her gown and to estimate their costs. Then they wander off to speculate on the bride's age and the groom's prospects.

Now, sitting in state in Park's Funeral Home, Momma closed her eyes and summoned up the memory of those faint lovely waltzes played by the Budapest Quartet of Grand Street, all strings, hired not by the hour but for the entire night.

She saw again the dressed-up, festive people who had come to dance at her wedding, and she swayed her head a little in time to the rhythm.

As she opened her eyes, the doors of the waiting room also opened and people slowly began to come in, the first of whom was her cousin Aaron, the intellectual, like a ghost of that long-ago wedding, tall and emaciated, bony-faced, gray.

Aaron was still busy "taking courses," registering every September and January at City College even though he was more than fifty years old. He always thought he knew everything better than anyone else in the world. He was an absolute nothing—and valued absolutely nothing—except his own words.

He was wearing a black sack suit, the vest buttoned up like it was winter. His pants hung from his thin body as if they were trying to get away. The others who'd entered stayed far from her in the corners, but he walked straight over and bent to brush his thin mouth against her cheek. His eyes, behind the wire-rimmed glasses, were red. A tear glimmered in one eye as he spoke.

"Eva, I'm so sorry. I'm so sorry."

That was kind of him. Momma nodded her appreciation. Maybe, so late in life, he was becoming a *mensch*?

"That's the way the world is," he continued, standing very close and looking down on her. "Too many people."

Now she wished that he would go away. Just go away. But he didn't.

His eyes checked around to see who else was
listening to him. Disappointment: no one was close
enough to hear, only Momma. "If you want to know
what the real trouble is, that's it. People! A population explosion that's worse than any bomb. More
people get born. Fewer die. So it has to be solved *this*
way. Surely you've heard about Malthus? You know
about the population explosion?" He peered down at
her face avidly, ready to devour her for her igno-
rance.

What he had to say was always *so* important.

"Take the larger view. Think about it this way.
He died for mankind. The world just doesn't have
enough food for all its people."

For you the world has enough food, you donkey, Momma thought. You always were and you'll
always be a donkey. You should eat grass.

She looked past him.

He moved off to explode his populations in
the face of Momma's fancy sister, Lily, and Lily's
husband, Irving. Momma watched finicky Irving already pushing up his sleeve as Aaron began to talk,
Irving studying his watch and a second later checking it again. Sunday was the busiest day in the dry
goods store and Irving could not bear to be far from
the action.

It pleased Momma that Irving was stuck listening to Aaron. They deserved one another. She

smiled to herself. Ever since Lily and Irving had argued over who should write the check at Ben's bar mitzvah, she had hated Irving. Go on, talk, she willed Aaron silently. Talk your head off.

Lily was listening to Aaron now, nodding her freshly curled hair. Momma could see by those tight sculpture-curls that this was a new permanent. So even though Lily *had* loved Ben and *was* sorry, that didn't stop her from rushing out to get her hair done. Quite the contrary. Lily believed that to be unfashionable or shabby or poor was a disgrace. That was why she had so little to do with her family. Lily was ashamed of all of them.

Momma was approached by two young women who seemed vaguely familiar. They were not relatives, that she knew.

Both were grossly fat. Their chemicaled jet hair was bouffanted high in beehives and trimmed with tiny, black-velvet ribbon bows. Hurrying up to Momma, they kissed her noisily.

"We're very sorry, Mrs. Greenfield. We really are. We really really are."

She looked at them, bewildered.

"You don't remember us, Mrs. Greenfield? You don't? You don't recall us from the store? The twins—Cheryl and Beryl Stein?"

Momma remembered them. And then, their voices tripped up the scale in triumph.

"Not Stein any more, of course." Titters.

"I remember you."

"Our folks couldn't leave the store on a Sunday. Sunday morning is the biggest appetizing morning, you know. Ma wanted to come anyway but Pa wouldn't let her. Sunday is also the biggest funeral day. If you knew the important funerals they had to miss in their lives—"

It was Cheryl doing the talking. She was the brighter one, and when she waited on you in the store she weighed her finger with the heavy diamond ring on it with every quarter pound of lox.

Beryl waited until her sister was finished and then put in her two cents' worth. "We came to *represent* the store."

"It wasn't necessary," Momma said and closed her eyes.

The twins stood there uncomfortably. They had never liked this woman who watched the scale so closely, as if someone was going to cheat her. But Ben was from the neighborhood and they thought they ought to pay their last respects. "That's the leas' we can do," they'd told one another and their husbands. "That's the leas'." They felt excited, ennobled by their attendance here today. Now they sidestepped away from Momma and scooted out so they wouldn't have to make any more conversation with her.

Shushing one another repeatedly, a large

group entered all together, in pairs, as if a teacher had lined them up. About thirty people. Some of the women were Italianers or Puerto Ricans, Momma could tell by their dark dresses and their black stockings and head kerchiefs. And some of them had dark skins.

Sol's shop.

Every single worker in the factory must have come. To give up a Sunday to come here was very nice of them, very considerate. A man wearing a black homburg gathered all these newcomers off to one side of the doorway, and then he approached Momma, limping, for his right leg was stiff.

"Mrs. Greenfield—" His voice was heavy with importance— "on behalf of all of us in Acme Custom-Tailored Pants, I'm now addressing you. To tell you how sorry we are about your tragic loss. May I say, personally, that Sol is like a brother to me."

Dazed, Momma followed these extravagant words. Surely this was Mr. Sternberg.

"I have six brothers and Sol is to me like the seventh. No less. You have given your son in the defense of your flag and you must be very proud. Sad, but proud. If my son were called this way to the Great Beyond, I know that I would feel that way."

Mr. Sternberg, Sol's boss?

Who else could it be with that limp? Today, in the undertaker's parlor, he was like a brother. All the years he had sucked Sol's blood. What kind of son was he talking about? What did he knew from sons? He had one divorced daughter, a bargain, a drinker. So what kind of son could he send to the Great Beyond?

Every night for more than twenty years, Momma had heard about this man: his bad leg, his stinginess over pennies, his fancy wife with the pencil eyebrows—one day Mrs. Sternberg had stopped at the factory to wash up and Sol reported that, washed, she looked like a honeydew melon, so fancy was she without the eyebrows.

Looking Mr. Sternberg over now, Momma was disappointed. He was so—ordinary. She had imagined that a boss would be grander.

How kind of the Italianers and the Puerto Ricans to come! They were family people, homeloving like the Jews. So much black clothing; they had plenty of tragedy of their own.

Momma smoothed the skirt of her gray print dress on her thighs and did her best not to laugh in big-shot Sternberg's face. Not *her* son. *She* had not given *her* son for her country. None of them knew it but *he* was not in that box. Not even Aaron, the smart one, Aaron with the Methuselah population explosions, not even he knew.

Ike came in with his wife. He came right to Momma and took her hand and wrung it then turned away, weeping, his paunchy face contorted with sorrow.

"It's all right, Ike," Momma said, wanting to comfort him because he, of them all, loved Ben. He had supplied the crack-eggs over the years to make the boy strong, and he had encouraged Ben to play baseball. Yes, Ike truly cared.

Fanny bent forward to kiss Momma and Momma inhaled perfume and was instantly resentful. Light was Fanny's head that she had nothing to think about but how she smelled at a funeral.

"Ike," Momma wondered, "you closed the store for the morning?"

"Not for the morning. I closed for the day. For my own nephew's funeral—he should rest his sweet head in peace—for this I shouldn't shut up my shop? I'm not Big-Shot Irving. And even he, I see, gave up dry goods for three hours today."

Ike stopped, numbed by grief.

Then he exploded.

"Only one uncle doesn't stop for a nephew's funeral. Only one uncle continues business as usual. Uncle Sam!"

"Shah, Ike," Fanny scolded. "Lower your voice."

"I said a lie?"

"No. But you don't have to yell and carry on. What good will it do? Think what you like but don't make trouble here."

"You're wrong! It must be said out loud. It must be understood."

At the top of his voice he bellowed, "Uncle Sam does business as usual while we come here to bury one of his murdered nephews. And all over America there are others. God alone knows how many others!"

Lily broke away from her group and hurried toward him. "Stop that at once," she snapped "You want people to think you're a subversive? A Commie?"

Ike stared at her. "What are you talking about? I own my own business. I pay taxes. Why are you making foolish charges with your big mouth? A Commie? Me? That's a laugh."

"The only people I know who talk this way are Communists," Lily said, glaring at him. "They're the ones who complain all the time about *Uncle Sam* and *Business as Usual*. Nothing is ever right in this country for them."

"Don't sing The Star Spangled Banner to me, Lily. I'm as good a citizen as you are any day—"

"It is time, dear friends," interposed the firm voice of Lieb, the Undertaker, "time for the mourners and the relatives who are not next-of-kin to take their places in the chapel inside. It is time for all of us to bid our last farewell to the dear departed."

"Thank God!" Lily was the first one through the doors and out of the waiting room.

NINETEEN

The chapel was half empty.

The first row, not yet occupied, was for the immediate family. Their close relatives were already seated right behind. But then there was a gap of many vacant rows, a no-man's land. The last section was spottily occupied: occasional family groups huddled together; Mr. Sternberg and his workers; elderly women in kerchiefs were in seats alone here and there; men from Sol's shul sat in pairs and threesomes; a group of Boy Scouts in shorts, one of them holding a furled flag, filled up two rear rows; way in the back and far to the left near the Fire Exit sat the two plump young women, chewing gum. People tended to take seats as far from the front as possible, as far from the soldiers standing at attention and the flag-covered box and the reserved rows.

Lieb waited for the them all to settle down before he ushered in the immediate family.

The next-of-kin always came down the aisle to their seats last in solemn procession.

Then Lieb would let the rabbi in through the concealed door in the wall up front. He would have gladly supplied the tasteful black robe for the officiant but he knew Rabbi Zoffar would not wear it.

The soldiers stood rigid. The coughing and noseblowing and footscraping finally abated.

In they came, the father bent and red-eyed, shuffling into the first row, end-seat, and bobbling there as if he were about to fall forward. Then the mother, remote, limping with a slackness to sit beside her husband, eyes sunken, hair a disordered yellow-gray, age's caricature of woman.

Lieb opened the door and the rabbi entered, a small man, neat in his navy blue suit, his wispy gray beard somehow at odds with his round, unwrinkled and untroubled face. The rabbi maintained an expression of constant beatitude. Sol believed that this serenity was due to the rabbi's inner spiritual peace though there was a dissident faction in the shul which attributed the rabbi's sleekness to overeating and chronic self-care. He did have a passion for food, for *chulent* and chicken livers chopped with onions and chicken fat.

Chanting in Hebrew, Rabbi Zoffar paused occasionally to translate into meticulous rabbinical English.

"*Shma Yisroel: Adonoi elohenu, Adonoi echod.*

"Hear O Israel: the Lord is our God, the Lord

is One.

"Blessed be His name whose glorious kingdom is forever and ever."

Sol sobbed uncontrollably.

Momma sat beside him, silent. Knowing that Ben was not in that box, she bided her time letting her mind leap ahead to the day when he would be home again. These ceremonies today here on Eastern Parkway had nothing whatever to do with her. She could just sit quietly and patiently because she had faith.

Sol, watching her, waited for the crack, for the fissure of death that had rended him to reach her and to split that terrible apathy. What he saw and heard made him weep harder.

"I once saw a woman with a beard like the rabbi's," she whispered.

He stared at her. She seemed to him a stranger.

"*And thou shalt love the Lord thy God with all thine heart, and with all thy soul, and with all thy might. And these words which I command thee this day shall be upon thine heart: and thou shalt teach them diligently unto thy children and shalt talk of them when thou sittest in thine house, and when thou walkest by the way, and when thou liest down, and when thou risest up. And thou shalt bind them for a sign upon thine hand, and they shalt be for thee frontlets between thine eyes. And thou shalt write them upon the doorposts of thy house and upon thy gates.*"

Momma sat there, placid.

Sol, beside her, knew terror. Her strength had no base. She was not taking comfort from anything being offered here. What then? What unknown remedy kept her still, kept her shrieks silent, her despair denied?

Gypsies, Sol thought, and he was afraid. Tea leaves. Coney Island comfort.

On went the rabbi, as he was required, on and on and on.

That the rabbi liked and respected him, Sol knew. He listened gratefully to the ceremonial words. Rabbi Zoffar always understood what was appropriate and gave members what they were entitled to. Sol, a member of the burial society for thirty years, appreciated the rabbi's solemnity. Ceremony was essential; ritual was required. The rabbi would not push Greenfield's only son into the grave: one, two, three.

Now the rabbi began his oration and in it he offered up each phrase grandly, individually, almost exclusively. On such occasions when he spoke formally, he brought his words forth like newly excavated treasures from his private spiritual mine.

"A bar mitzvah boy who read Talmud—a young tree cut down at the height of its blooming—an Eagle Scout who loved the stars and stripes too much—a diligent high school student—an all-American lad." The rabbi paused after that beautiful word *lad*. "He will intercede for you, for his beloved mother and his respected father and for all his dear relatives and friends."

Ike shifted in his seat restlessly. "Enough already, rabbi," he muttered. "Enough."

The rabbi appeared to be carried away by his own words.

"And sometimes God in his righteousness asks much of us. He demands sacrifices of us. His way is not easy. Did he not send Abraham up into the mountains of the land of Moriah and bid him give his son Isaac there as a burnt offering? It was hard enough, this task he gave Abraham. Then why did he make him go up into the mountains? Why not just allow him to make the sacrifice down in the valley? Abraham was already an old man.

"Because God did not want to make religion an easy thing.

"And now I ask you to look around this half-empty chapel today with me. Where are our brothers in Judaism? Where is the membership to pay homage? Here before us lies a Jewish son. He died for his country. We few have come to do him honor, but the rest of his brethren, like Abraham, are up in the mountains. The Catskill mountains! They go for the weekend; they go Friday night after sundown; they go Saturday morning.

"Are these the mountains God summons us
to?

"I tell you NO. He did not mean Pine Lodge or
Grossingers. It's a shame before the world for Jews to
behave this way."

Ike glared at the rabbi. What was he running,
a membership drive?

"*Yiskadal v'yiskadash shmey rabo*
B'olmo divro...."

The soldiers raised their guns. For one terrible
moment it look like they were going to fire at the
imitation stars in the ceiling, but no. they shouldered
the guns snappily. They slow-marched beside the
coffin. Meanwhile, the rabbi slipped out through the
door in the wall.

The two young women in back waddled to the
Fire Exit. They found that door locked, and much as
they hated to, they had to scurry right in front of the
coffin because they were in a hurry and needed to get
home.

Quickly, the few limousines were filled and
lined up. Lieb appeared at the open window of the
lead car. "All comfortable, folks?" he asked. "All
satisfactory, Mr. Greenfield?"

Sol leaned forward. "You'll get your money
from the shul secretary, Lieb."

"Money is the farthest thing from my mind,"
Lieb protested.

"I'm sure," Sol said, rolling up the window. "Can't we go?" he asked the driver.

"Sorry. I have to follow the hearse."

Sol nodded and then sank back in the seat and kept his eyes shut until the small cortege moved off. That way he didn't have to look at Lieb's face again.

TWENTY

They drove from the cemetery to Grant Street in the big Cadillac limousine. Momma was impressed by its huge, well-appointed depths. On the way there her mind had been elsewhere, but now she took notice. Millionaires rode around in cars like this: the Rockefellers, the Carnegies, and probably the Duchess of Windsor.

This was the way *big* people traveled.

The gray upholstery was sleek, velvety. She slid her hand along the fabric timidly. Her grainy skin caught against it.

Silken velvet. It could cushion a throne.

The car glided along noiselessly.

Rollo's Cadillac had traveled the same easy way, as if it were floating on smooth still water. Of course, in the open car you got the wind and the fresh air. This sealed Cadillac was more elegant. More formal.

Driving back with Rollo had made Momma feel young. Now she smiled at the memory. Perhaps

it was the radio with the dance music that had done
it.

Suddenly she wondered, did this limousine
have a radio? Or did they manufacture special silent
models for funerals?

"Is there a radio?" she asked.

"A what?" Sol did not think he had heard
right.

"Nothing. I was just thinking out loud."

Sol *had* heard the question, and he was not
reassured by her disclaimer.

Where was her mind wandering? Over what
strange and lonely barren path had she traveled
during these last months? Where was she?

In what Gehenna?

How could he bring her back to this world?

To this terrible funeral?

Sol had no desire to speak. His thoughts were
private. His thoughts were unspeakable.

He was remembering Ben and the guns; Ben,
who never in his life had a gun for a toy because
weapons meant violence and Momma was afraid of
violence.

Ben, back there in the grave under the raw
brown earth.

Sol's thighs and legs were trembling. Soon,
soon he too would be in the grave.

Without army guns.

Whoever thought up the idea of firing guns over the grave of a dead soldier? It added insult to injury.

This Jewish funeral was essential. Ben could not have been left there on the other side of the world to lie among strangers.

Maybe the secretary of the shul would save two places near Ben.

Unlikely.

If a man could not afford to buy a family plot, he had to take his next wherever and whenever it came.

Still, it would be nice to be together.

Sol's nose was running. He took out his handkerchief and blew hard. He could cry and blow his nose forever. Who would notice?

What good was it to cry?

Did the President cry?

No.

Instead the President sent mail: big manila envelopes that didn't fit inside the mailbox, condolences with cardboard backing in them and warnings to the postman not to fold or spindle; condolences with the signatures embossed on them to look like real handwriting.

What did the President care that back there they had buried *the remains* of one boy?

Sol's whole body quivered when his mind

touched that terrible phrase.

The remains.

Of adolescence.

Of hopes and dreams.

To die in such a horrible way. Why? What did the American son of Solomon Greenfield have to do with Korea?

Had life not been hard enough all during those dark cold years in Brooklyn that they should take his only beloved son away and kill him?

He knew he should worry more about Communism. The newspapers constantly told him so.

The Jewish War Veterans told him so too, regularly, for he was a Life Member and went to monthly meetings.

Senator Joseph McCarthy told him so.

And J. Edgar Hoover had been spreading the word for years.

Sol was no lunatic pacifist. He had willingly gone to fight in 1917. He loved America with all his heart. When it needed protection, it could count on him.

It was the best country in the world with the best kind of government.

No question.

But for all of that, Ben was dead. For nothing.

Not for America. For nothing.

That was what hurt so, and he pondered it

again and again, and still his mind echoed with the epitaph that truly should go on the gravestone: "For nothing!"

He began to talk. Empty talk.

"Summer traffic is heavy....It's very hot already....August will be murder....Rabbi Zoffar is getting old; seventy-six is no spring chicken....He doesn't do many funerals these days, but for Ben's he wouldn't think of not coming....He used to walk from the entrance gates of the cemetery to the shul burial grounds, but today he had to be driven in...."

Momma did not respond to any of this, so he asked her directly, "Did you notice that the rabbi came all the way into the cemetery in a car?"

No answer. She didn't seem to know that he was speaking to her.

Sol stopped talking.

He had decided with the rabbi that though Ben had been dead more than thirty days, the family would pay full respects and rend their garments. So, at the graveside, the rabbi had made a small cut with his knife on the collar of Sol's shirt and then Sol, himself, had torn the cloth properly.

But Momma had not allowed the rabbi to cut cloth.

She had made a dreadful scene, refusing the rite despite the rabbi's severe words.

It was true that the years of poverty had made

her stingy, but Sol knew that she didn't care that much about a dress.

How could she carry on so?

Had she no respect for their child lying there before them in the soft brown earth?

Momma had absolutely refused to tear her clothes!

The rabbi, standing by the grave, had rebuked her, but she would not obey. What did she care about the knife in his hand? He couldn't boss her.

The rabbi, believing her strange behavior to be the madness of extreme grief, tried to scold her back to normality.

"It is forbidden to grieve excessively for the dead. Three days are allowed for weeping, seven for mourning, and thirty for abstaining from wearing ironed clothes or cutting the hair. Those are the laws."

She looked up into the blue summer sky, averting her face from him. A wild impulse to hum something gay seized her and it was all she could do to keep her mouth shut, her throat silent.

The rabbi did not give up easily.

"He who mourns in excess will have cause to mourn for another death. This is *your son* for whom we are gathered here. He died—" The rabbi paused and sent forth a piteous sigh; once in a hundred funerals, once in a thousand, a rabbi had to deal with such a tragic case.

"He died only the One Above knows when, maybe a year ago, maybe more, maybe less. It is written that the children of Israel wept for Moses in the plains of Moab thirty days and they were indeed days of weeping and mourning. So thirty days was sufficient mourning for Moses, whom the Lord knew face to face.

"I say to you now, rend your clothing and sit the week of mourning with your husband, and you'll know a little peace at last." The rabbi's tone was not unkind; he was almost pleading.

Momma pursed her lips and stared at him.

That was her answer.

Abruptly, the rabbi snapped his penknife shut. He pocketed the knife then finished his tasks at the graveside quickly. In one minute it would all be over.

Again he tried to remind her of her duty.

"Our rabbis say if one of the family has died, the entire family should show sorrow. To what can this be compared? To a vault made of stones. When one stone trembles, all of them tremble at the same time...."

Her face was a mask of defiance shutting the rabbi and his words out. Not only *his* words, Sol thought sorrowfully, but the wisdom of the sages!

"Enough, Rabbi," Ike said softly.

Rabbi Zoffar turned, amazed at this presumption.

"My sister has suffered enough. Let's bring this to an end," Ike begged.

Agreeing with Ike that they'd all had as much as they could bear, Sol was, nonetheless, astonished at his brother-in-law. To tell the rabbi to stop took courage. Ike had truly loved Ben; Ike was much more than he seemed; Ike was a *mensch*!

"Fill your shoes with earth before you leave here," the rabbi ordered. Then he raised his hands in front of his chest and flung them outward, dismissing everyone. He took a step away then turned back.

"Greenfield, I am deeply sorry." He embraced Sol. "Mrs. Greenfield, I am deeply sorry."

"Rabbi, why don't you call my husband *mister*? *Mister* Greenfield? It's so much more dignified."

He shook his head, and, without another word, he made his way to his car.

TWENTY-ONE

Curious neighbors watched from the stoops and windows as the landlady—she whose son had returned safely from war in 1946—came up from her basement bearing a gallon jug of water so the mourners could rinse their hands.

Oh how Momma was tempted to grab the bottle and douse the witch in her own water and tell her, "Not my son either! Not my Ben!" But she kept herself quiet.

When *he* came home, then everyone would know. Then there would be time enough for triumph. Soon. Soon....

She allowed a sprinkle of water to dampen her hands.

Sol, weak and feeling peculiarly shrunken in his blue suit coat and torn shirt—as if his clothes had grown too big for him in the graveyard—washed himself carefully, mindful that nothing from there was to be brought into the house.

Then Ike, sagging, weary, his tan summer suit

powdered with the gray dust of the grave, spritzed himself from the jug, lavishly, sloppily.

Fanny, already washed, was in the dark hall upstairs, waiting. She had hurried ahead to gather some fruit crates for the mourners to sit on.

"I brought one apple box," she chattered at them from up above. Her blondined hair led them in the darkness like a torch. "Apple boxes are best. Whenever we sit *shiva* in my family, God forbid, we use only apple boxes but they're so popular, it's necessary to grab them in advance. They're strong like iron. I could only find one today, so the other one is from grapefruits." She pointed to the slatted lesser crate.

"That's why all the grapefruits are damaged," Momma said. "They're pushed in open crates. Even Sunkist. You wouldn't think when a grapefruit costs so much it would be packed carelessly. But in these times, who cares for the customer?"

Oranges and grapefruits today?

Shopping lists during *shiva*?

Who would ever understand women? Sol unlocked the door and they were now back in their living room pitifully shabby in the afternoon sunlight.

Removing his shoes, Sol sank down on the grapefruit crate which creaked but did not split. Momma edged between the two crates into the kitchenette and stood there looking through the window at the great oak tree so strong and permanent, so green and cool in the summer's heat.

"Sit on the apple box, Sol. I'm not sitting."

"Why not?"

"I'm not tired."

"Take your shoes off and sit. It's a sin to wear shoes now."

She stifled a yawn.

Pressing on his eyelids as if he could seal them forever from the sight of trouble, Sol tried to focus on what had to be done. He rose and went to the closet to get bed sheets.

What was wrong with her?

What could he do with her?

He didn't know.

Only one thing he knew: the mirrors should have been covered. Before the funeral, the mirrors should all have been shrouded or Ben's soul might appear in any one of them. That was Momma's responsibility and the sin would be on her head.

Averting his eyes, he began to drape the tarnished glass.

"Sit." Fanny took the sheet from his hands. "I'll do it."

"The glass in the bathroom too, Fanny, please."

Fanny had brought the funeral meal in a large, tan, wicker basket with the word *Calypso* embroidered in red raffia on the side. Once she'd covered the mirrors, she began to unpack the food bringing forth tomatoes, lettuce and hard-boiled eggs.

"Grade A guaranteed," Ike assured them.

Momma sniffed in a decidedly hostile way.

She was remembering a certain other Grade A egg.

Ike looked at her questioningly.

From the basket, Fanny unpacked a round, seeded rye bread and a stick of sweet butter, and, finally, a large thermos of coffee.

The mourners ate in silence, Sol on the mourner's box and Momma standing all the while by her window, calm, her clothing intact.

Soon after he was finished, Sol went to lie down in the bedroom. Momma remained standing in the kitchenette. As Fanny began to gather up the debris of the meal, Ike got up and wandered into the small bedroom that had been Ben's.

The yellowing Boy Scout snapshots were still taped onto the cracked walls. Against the footboard of the bed rested his bicycle, its decorative squirrel tail looking ratty and limp. Near the bike pedals neatly piled were roller skates, a football, and a peeling catcher's mitt. When Ben was alive there had never been such order in this room; Ben was a whirlwind, always playing, running, teasing, perpetual motion.

Ike sat down on the lumpy mattress.

A minute later, Momma was in the doorway.

"Why do you sit in here?"

"It's peaceful. I was thinking."

A flicker of pain moved her sunken mouth.

"You should do your thinking elsewhere."

"For what I'm thinking, this is the right place."

Anger flickered in her eyes. "What are you thinking?"

"That you are out of touch. You don't know what's really going on. You don't *believe* Ben is dead. That's what I'm thinking in here. That you don't truly *understand* that we put Ben in his grave today."

A secretive smile twisted her face, frightening Ike. Still, he persisted. "You *don't* believe he's dead, do you?"

His voice was thunder in her ears.

"Do you?"

She had to pull her collar far down from her neck and hold it there so she could breathe.

What answer should she give?

She couldn't jeopardize Ben's life by lying, by echoing yes, yes, I know he's dead...when he wasn't dead.

Turning aside for an instant, she rubbed her forehead where the intellectual powers, the perceptive and moral powers of the brain lay, according to Zoe's phrenology drawing. Momma needed those powers to come to her aid.

No answers came to her. She turned back to him, quivering with anger and outrage.

This brother of hers, this stranger with the red pouchy cheeks, the untidy black hair, and the gray eyes shadowed by unhealthy patches—this gross busybody—how dare he? How dare this egg-candler challenge her?

BEN WAS HER SON.

Motherhood was woman's greatest achievement. She was a mother and so she was entitled to respect!

What kind of world had this become where a younger brother could say such things to an older sister?

Some things were not a brother's business. They were private. Like matters between a husband and wife. Personal matters. *Strictly private.*

She would stop him now.

"Don't worry about me. I took care of things. I made a small investment that will bring us all happiness. That's all I did."

"Do you believe Ben's dead?" Ike hammered at her. "Do you?"

"Who gave you the right to question me?"

"Tell me! Do you or do you not believe he's dead? *Answer the question.*" He bellowed this at her so loud that Fanny came running in from the living room.

"Ike—Eva—what's wrong?"

"Nothing." Momma tossed her head in dismissal, but Fanny did not go away.

"Stop with the questions, Ike. You should have more respect in this house of sorrow."

Now her brain was beginning to handle things.

House of sorrow was clever because it didn't force her to say that Ben was alive or make her pretend that she thought he was dead. Ike would surely leave her alone now.

Wouldn't it be glorious if Ben chose today to come home?

What a surprise! To return on his own funeral day like Tom Sawyer.

Oh Ben, Ben. Come home. Come today and show all the smart alecks.

"Sol tells me you go to Coney Island a lot," Ike said softly. "You find something there? You have something good there—in Coney Island?"

She didn't like his tone, his manner; he was insinuating nasty things. "So?"

"You don't have anyone in Coney Island," he went on. "You hate Coney Island."

"I have friends."

"Aah," he seized on that. "What kind of friends? Fortunetellers? Maybe Gypsies have been comforting you?"

"I'm not entitled to comfort?"

"Who says no? Of course you're entitled. But not from crooks. If they suck money out of you, they'll disappear. They'll take your savings and fly away like the birds."

Momma felt contempt for him. He was so ignorant. "I don't like to say this to you, Ike, because you are my own flesh and blood. But you don't know who or what you're talking about. Mind your own damn business. You'll be better off."

He moved into the doorway, hands braced on either side of the frame, blocking passage. "If you don't tell me everything, I'll wake Sol and you'll have to tell him."

Both he and Fanny were staring at her now just as the Boardwalk crowd had stared at Madame Myra, in fascination and disbelief. Also fear; they were afraid of what they couldn't understand.

Momma turned away from them and hunched her back slightly, hiding. "Why should I answer questions like a criminal? Who are you? Who is *she* to hear my private business?"

"We're your family." Fanny was all sweetness. "You know we care about you. If you gave money to Gypsies, please tell us. We want to help you."

The need in her to escape was desperate, but there was only one doorway out of the room and Ike was blocking it.

"Never mind your help. Don't mix in what doesn't concern you. You don't know everything in this world." Momma took a step toward Ike hoping that he would step aside.

He didn't budge.

"Listen," he said gently, and he put out a restraining hand, "Ben is dead. We all loved him very much, but dead is dead. If anyone told you anything different and they took your money, say good-bye to it. They stole it. Because Ben is dead. *Dead!* Fanny and I know about Gypsies, about fortunetellers. Over the years they swindled plenty of our customers. They have no pity. Hear what I say. Ben is dead. You loved him very much, but he's dead."

"I don't take advice from egg-candlers and their bleached wives."

"I don't candle eggs—not for years."

"Maybe you should. It's what you're good for."

Ike was not to be put off by insults.

"Show me your bankbook. If it's all right, if your savings are still in the bank, I'll apologize and we'll forget all this."

"My bankbook is my business. Some nerve. Do I ask to see your bankbook?"

"It's also Sol's business," Fanny butted in. "I'll go wake him and tell him."

"It's only my business." Momma began to weep. "I scrimped to save the little money we have. I beg you. Don't tamper with what doesn't concern you. You'll spoil all my good work, all my trouble, all my trips on Ben's behalf. All the carfare, all the shopping, everything."

She lashed out at them. "You think you know everything? You don't know anything!"

"We know that you've been going to Coney Island to the Gypsies," Fanny said. She was relentless. "We know they must have all your money."

"Please—I've suffered so much. Please leave me alone."

"I know you've suffered—" Ike began, but she stopped him.

"How do *you* know? Are you a mother?"

"Get the bankbook or we'll have Sol in here."

"What do you want of me? Leave me alone," Momma implored. "Oh God, what am I going to do?"

Awkwardly she began to bend a knee, to get down. "I beg you on—"

Ike grabbed her elbow, bracing her upright. "Stop it, Eva."

"*My name is Momma. I am Ben's Momma and you know it.*"

"Get the bankbook." Fanny's voice was harsh. "You don't want us to see it, we won't. Ike will go down and phone the police. Then he'll get a cab and we'll just ride over to headquarters. You can talk to them private there. We won't know anything. If they're satisfied that everything is kosher, we'll come right back here. No one will say one word to you any more. Not one word."

"You promise? You promise that if it turns out my friend is a good and honest friend—with special powers—you'll leave us alone? And you won't tell Sol?"

"I promise." Fanny's hand was on her heart. "Otherwise we'll bring the police here."

The police?

Here in the house?

What could she do? She had to put them off till she could think of something. Maybe Ben would arrive suddenly. God would surely help her. The thing to do was to keep the bankbook out of their hands.

"All right. You bullied me so much, I'll go. Too many arguments here. Too much trouble." She paused, embarrassed. "Fanny, I'm sorry for what I said about your hair."

"It's all right. It is dyed. I never pretended not."

"Still—some things a nice person doesn't say. I'll just go wash my face and comb my hair and get ready."

Ike moved out of the doorway to let her get by.

"Go with her, Fanny," he whispered. "She shouldn't be alone. I'll wake Sol and tell him we're going."

When the bathroom door was closed, Ike walked into the bedroom where his brother-in-law lay. Sol, on his back on top of the patchwork bedspread. was breathing noisily, his arm shielding his eyes from the light. He stirred.

"Ike? Already time for prayers?"

"No. Listen, Sol. I'm sorry. I came to tell you Fanny and I are taking Momma to the police."

"Now? Today? Why?"

"We think the Gypsies took her for whatever they could get."

"She dasn't. She's not allowed to leave the house, Ike. We're in mourning."

"Her shoes are on her feet. Her clothing is not torn. She's not sitting on a box. *She's* not in mourning because she doesn't believe Ben is dead."

"She's not permitted to go anywhere."

"The Gypsies will disappear with your savings. You want that?"

His whole life had come to utter defeat. Sol felt numb. Nothing that could happen mattered any more.

"Go. See if the police can make her understand that she should sprinkle earth in her shoes and sit *shiva* on her box."

"About the Gypsies, Sol. You aren't supposed to know anything. I promised her."

"Know?" Sol repeated wearily. "What do I know?"

TWENTY-TWO

When the taxi stopped, Ike jumped out of the front seat to open the rear door near the sidewalk, but Momma would not go out that way. She wanted to show him how angry she was. Fanny had to climb over her then she slid over to the far side, opened that door and descended into the middle of the street.

"Keep track of what you spend," she told Ike. "I'll pay you back. I don't need you to pay my fare."

Limping to the curb, she put a foot up and then stopped to look around.

Broome Street.

What were they doing on Broome Street with dirty, ugly buildings all around them? The buildings seemed to be largely boarded-up or shuttered factories and warehouses. Probably they were factories closed because it was Sunday.

Not one person on the street besides them.

Who else but lunatics would come down here on a Sunday? Her whole life she had managed to stay away from any business with the police, and now her own brother was getting her mixed up with them. What should she do?

The officer on guard in the lobby listened to Ike for a minute and then directed them: "Pickpocket and Confidence Squad—seventh floor."

"Nobody picked my pocket," Momma protested, as Fanny tugged her toward the elevator.

"Nobody picked my pocket," she repeated louder. "I don't even have pockets. I sew them up so the garments won't tear. Where are we going?"

"The Confidence Squad handles fortune tellers," Fanny said.

"I have confidence in my friend." Momma pursed her lips and stepped away from Fanny.

Mrs. Know-It-All.

Yes, it was all Fanny's fault. The whole business with the bankbook. It was her idea that Momma should come here with her bankbook in her hand. Ike could never think up such a thing by himself.

Who would have believed that Momma—Eva Greenfield—a plain Jewish housewife, could have such an adventure?

And what made Fanny such a Number One Big Shot? Just because she was married to Ike, did that make her so smart?

Momma was working herself up to some really scathing remarks when the elevator arrived on the seventh floor and the doors slid open.

192

They were in a big, barren, shabby area much like a warehouse loft. Strange that the greatest city in the world could not afford a better police headquarters.

A gray-haired, portly Irisher—Momma knew immediately by his face that his people had come during the potato famine—spoke briefly to Ike and Fanny. Then he headed toward Momma.

"Mrs. Greenfield? I am Detective Lanihan." He smiled, and the smile made him look both distinguished and friendly. Crooking his arm, he offered it to her in the old fashioned way.

"Come and meet my colleagues." He walked her over to an open office door leaving Fanny and Ike behind.

In they went.

"I'd like to present Detective Vitale." He pointed to a dark, handsome young man. "And this is Detective Reilly—Peggy Reilly." A trim brunette in a stunning brown silk suit stood just inside the doorway next to the massive file cabinets.

"Call me Peggy," she said pleasantly. "I'll bet I'm the first woman detective you've ever met, Mrs Greenfield. Right?"

"Right. But I never met any men detectives either. I never had anything to do with the police before in my life."

"Very sensible," Lanihan said. "I try to have

as little as possible to do with them myself."

Momma relaxed a little. Everything she'd ever heard about detectives, that they were tough and brutal and dirty-mouthed, was not true here.

These people were quite pleasant.

"We'll settle down in here for our talk," Lanihan said.

"Alone? Without my brother and his wife?"

"They'll wait for you out there. There's a bench for them to sit on. That's the deal. Peggy, will you shut the door."

He led Momma to a straight-backed chair beside the big desk. Then he went round to sit in the swivel chair while the other two detectives moved chairs close by, flanking Momma.

She looked around.

The office was big and bare like the rest of the building. The desk was oak, massive and old-fashioned. Green shades covered the huge windows. A frayed wall map was the single decoration, but Momma was not sure what it was a map of. Probably the city. Anyway it added a bit of color. The map and the desk gave the place a schoolroom look.

Lighting a cigarette, Lanihan settled back and crossed his legs. Peggy Reilly took a long pad of yellow paper from a leather briefcase.

Suddenly the three of them were alert and waiting. Momma could feel the tension in the air.

"All right, Mrs. Greenfield, what is it you have to tell us?" Lanihan began.

"Nothing, really." Momma smiled fondly. "Coming here was a foolish idea. It was not mine. It was my sister-in-law's. She and my brother are business people, retail business, they have a nice little store. You know business people. If they earn a good living, they think they know everything. We had a little family disagreement, so *they* decided that we should come down here and waste your time. Since it's their idea, why don't you ask them?" She smiled again, hoping that she had disarmed them.

Nothing happened. The three detectives continued to sit there looking at her.

"That your bankbook you're holding there, Mrs. Greenfield? Mind if I have a look?"

Lanihan was up, out of the chair and leaning over, his big hand spread out flat like a shovel, reaching forth over the desk before Momma could protect herself with all the reasons why he needn't bother. He scooped it away.

Settling back down into the well of his chair, he began to peruse it, to flip pages, reading, checking, going back, rechecking. He started to whistle softly. It was a familiar tune, Momma recognized from Sunday afternoon radio concerts. "Orpheus in the Underworld."

Such a cultured Irishman.

He handed the bankbook to his colleague, Vitale, who looked it over quickly, then turned it over to Peggy Reilly. She began to copy from it onto her pad.

Momma felt as if her stomach had dropped right out of her.

Detective Lanihan picked up the conversation. "What's the name of your Gypsy friend, Mrs. Greenfield?"

Smoothing her dress over her knees, Momma decided that she would answer only the questions that were not damaging to Ben. Or to Zoe. They could give her the third degree or even put her in jail, but she would be mighty careful about what she told them and what she held back.

A name, she decided, could do no harm.

"Zoe. Princess Zoe."

"Mmm. When did you first meet her?"

"Mother's Day. That's a big day in America. All my enemies should have such a day as I had. That's what I wish."

Next to her the pencil tracked across the yellow paper speedily, copying, copying.

All of this was terrible, yet, in a way, very flattering. They were hanging on to her every word. No important officials had ever paid her so much attention. She resolved to watch her grammar.

"I bet you walked into her store on Mother's

Day, and she just looked at you and read your mind perfectly."

How could he know? Momma gaped. "Who told you that?"

"Fortunetellers are his specialty," Vitale said. "He knows everything there is to know about them."

"Not quite everything." Lanihan tapped a pencil on the desk, his eyes on Momma. "She took one look at you—" he began, and then paused, putting his hand over his mouth.

Ha! The big shot detective wasn't so smart.

"Yes, she took a single look at you and told you that—*your son was missing!*" His last four words were sharp; they cut the air like pistol shots on a radio program.

She flinched.

"Sorry," he said. "No. I don't know everything," his manner was mild again. "But I do know that Princess Zoe promised to bring your son home." Then he sat up straight in his chair and looked compellingly at Momma. "Isn't that what she promised you? Safe? Your boy would come home to you safe?"

She was trapped.

"I—I—don't know," she faltered, "who's been telling you all my secrets." Her hands moved in her lap nervously smoothing her clothes. "You mustn't make trouble, Detective Lanihan. My brother swore you wouldn't make trouble if I came."

"We will not make trouble for you, Mrs. Greenfield."

"Good. Because the only reason I'm here is so you can tell those meddlers not to interfere. My bankbook is my own business. I want them to leave me alone."

"We're here to help you if we can, believe me. Now suppose you go over the bankbook with me and tell me how much money went to Princess Zoe and just how she was using it to help your son come home."

Momma had her bankbook back safe in her hands.

Lanihan rode his chair around the desk. Detective Vitale moved away to make room for him, so he was right next to Momma where he could read the figures with her.

She didn't want to in the worst way. "Must I do this?"

"We're the police," Lanihan said sternly. "Of course you must."

"I'll do my best to remember." She opened the bankbook. "This first hundred dollars—"

"Didn't you bring it to her with an egg all wrapped up in a man's handkerchief—white for purity?" Lanihan asked softly.

"Yes. But how—"

"And the Princess cracked the egg open and

198

there was something very ugly in it. Something re-
volting. Right?"

Momma shuddered. "Don't speak of it. Don't!"

He got up and went to open his desk drawer.
"Was it a devil's head like this?"

She shut her eyes.

The drawer slammed shut "All right, Mrs.
Greenfield, I've put it away."

He resumed his seat and was silent for a
minute. When she was looking at him again, bewildered, he spoke bluntly.

"I want you to try to understand that your
friend, Princess Zoe, is a crook."

Momma stood up.

She didn't have to listen.

She had done nothing wrong.

Men and women of little faith. That's what
they were.

"The reason I can tell you what she did—the
devil's head in the egg and the money and all the
rest—is that many crooked fortunetellers operate
this way. I'm going to show you exactly how they
work. Sit down, Mrs. Greenfield."

Momma did not obey.

"I know it's hard for you to believe, but Princess Zoe is no friend of yours. She's a crook, a ruth-
less, dangerous crook." He motioned for Momma to
take her seat again and waited.

She sat. "No matter what you or anyone else says, I believe she *is* my friend. She offered me more kind words and comfort—she was more interested in me and my suffering—than anyone else in my whole life. You're wasting your time. I believe in Princess Zoe."

"Let's go on with the bankbook. Next withdrawal."

"One thousand dollars."

"Let me guess. The spirits told the fortuneteller it was cursed money, so you would have to tear it up and flush it down the toilet." He looked at Momma eagerly. "Is that what happened to your money?"

"You're only partly right."

"Oh?" He sounded surprised. And intrigued.

"*She* flushed it down," Momma said. "I have bad feet and the toilet is upstairs so she saved me the walking up. But I did tear all the money."

"Too bad," he muttered.

Momma was totally bewildered. "What?"

"Too bad you did the tearing. I was hoping...."

"The fortuneteller wouldn't make a mistake like that," Vitale said. "She's a pro."

"You never know," Lanihan shrugged.

"What are you talking about?" Momma asked helplessly.

"We're talking about destroying legal tender. It's a crime. But hold up a minute. We skipped a step.

Before you tore the money you'd given her, you shut
your eyes and prayed. Right?"

"I did pray."

"That's when she substituted phony money
for what you handed her."

"No!" Momma denied emphatically. "No. I
saw what I was doing. It was *money* I tore up, my evil
money from the bank. I did it for him. Gladly. I'd do
it again. Even if it was a crime and I have to go to
jail...."

"Don't worry about that. I wish she'd done
the tearing. But except for the cover bills maybe, you
didn't tear real money," he reassured her. "Let's go
on. What was the next withdrawal from the bank,
Mrs. Greenfield?"

"Four thousand dollars."

He exhaled heavily. "That much? That's fast."
He looked at his colleagues. "Zoe was feeling confi-
dent, eh? She knew her customer."

Both detectives nodded.

"She put your four thousand dollars in a big
shopping bag with a live chicken. You shut your eyes
and prayed and she prayed too, good and loud. Then
the chicken squawked. And it was dead when she
dumped it out of the bag."

Momma didn't know what to say. He was
absolutely amazing.

He was clairvoyant too.

He could probably tell fortunes and help people just the way Zoe did. Except that no one would believe that an Irishman had second sight.

But Momma had always believed that there were special people in the world with extraordinary psychic perception. It was a fantastic coincidence to run into two, one right after the other, after waiting a whole lifetime.

He continued. "Next, she said she would burn your evil money. She got a garbage can and put the money on the bottom and pretty soon there were pretty white clouds of smoke rising. You probably smelled ammonia."

Momma remembered the smell but she kept the memory to herself.

"Hydrochloric acid and ammonia make terrific smoke."

"You are wrong. I saw her light the match. She burned it," Momma said positively.

Lanihan shook his dead. "Anything else?"

"A trifle. I paid two dollars and thirteen cents for the chicken so it would be my own chicken even though she did the buying. Between you and me, it wasn't that much of a chicken for that price, but what could I do? I couldn't bring a chicken on the subway from Williamsburg. I had to ask her to buy it for me. And when you send someone to shop for you, it always costs more."

"Two thirteen for a chicken," Vitale said to Peggy who wrote it down.

"You know what the fortuneteller's family ate for supper that night, Mrs. Greenfield? After you went home, you know what they cooked and ate? Your little chicken was their supper."

Momma stared at Lanihan.

She had misjudged him.

He wasn't too bright, that was for sure.

Who would eat a tainted chicken, a chicken that died in such a horrible way? Not even a cannibal.

"He's right," Detective Vitale said. "Why waste a perfectly healthy chicken?"

Momma turned on him. "So why did it die, if you're so smart? Tell me, why did it die? If you heard the shriek it gave, you wouldn't be making such jokes."

"It died because your Gypsy friend pressed on a heart muscle. It's a very old trick. And a very easy one."

"I don't believe you."

"Where is Zoe's *ofisa*?"

"You're not going to bother her—to arrest her? Ike promised—"

"No," Lanihan said. "I'm just wondering if she's still around."

"Sure she is. She lives there."

"Where?"

"West Twenty-third Street. Near the Boardwalk. The store with the cleanest windows. I think she cleans them with Glass Wax because water never gets glass so clean."

"When was the last time you saw her?"

"One month ago today, exactly."

"Mmm. She's gone," Vitale murmured.

"I'd be willing to bet on that," Lanihan agreed. "But let's check. We'll just send a patrol car cruising down that block. No one will disturb her, Mrs. Greenfield. Don't worry. The men will just drive by and see if the store is still occupied."

"You could take my word for it."

Peggy Reilly patted her arm.

"Send a car to look around," Lanihan told Vitale. "And tell the relatives in the hall outside that everything is under control."

Detective Vitale rose to go.

"Don't tell the bleached blond anything. She's not a blood relative. She's the big troublemaker."

"Tell the brother," Lanihan instructed.

That gave Momma some satisfaction.

"Any more to tell us, Mrs. Greenfield?"

"Well—you know everything else. This isn't exactly to do with money. I did buy new clothes for my son, pants and shoes, big sizes because he's grown and gained weight, thank God. I spent about thirty-five dollars. I even tucked shoe polish and a chamois cloth in the toes of the shoes for a surprise. Because the army emphasizes shined shoes. Mothers think of everything."

"Zoe's husband must be a big man. Heavyset," Lanihan observed. "Okay, Peggy. Can we have a total on that?"

"Five thousand one hundred thirty-seven dollars and thirteen cents."

"That sounds right to the penny," Momma agreed.

"We'll only ask one other thing of you today, Mrs. Greenfield," Lanihan said. "We have many pictures of fortunetellers in our file. If I showed them to you, do you think you could pick out your friend?"

Momma laughed. "Of course. I'd know her in a minute. But she won't be there. Why should she be in a police file? And even if her picture were there, it still wouldn't matter to me. I believe in her."

"Come along and we'll have a look."

There was an amazing collection of pictures. Momma went through them one by one, carefully. Each new photograph made her feel more positive; none of these people had she ever seen.

Then—one picture caught her eye. "It's a striking resemblance," she conceded.

Eagerly, Lanihan took it and studied it. After a long time, he began to page through the rest of the album, whistling his one Offenbach tune, until he came to something that stopped him. "You know this lady?"

Momma looked. It was—yet it wasn't—Zoe.

"She's had a nose job since then. It is your Zoe. That's one of her favorite names. She's also Hazel and Rose and Sybil. She *is* a princess, by the way. Her father is king of one of the big Gypsy tribes."

Because he was a detective, because he was another religion, because he was Irish and alien and he represented the law and the government, because of all these things, Momma did not dare to let go at him. She felt like hitting out, like thrashing them all.

"Where is my brother? Where is he and his fancy wife? Why did they have to tamper? Why couldn't they leave things alone? All my good work will be ruined. Those trips I made, and all those subway fares I wasted, and the hours and hours of riding the trains to Coney Island.

"Oh God! Why didn't all of you just leave things alone?"

"Eighteen arrests," Lanihan read from the file. "Eighteen arrests and not one single conviction."

"Ah!" Momma was triumphant. "I knew it. People always say bad things about Gypsies but they can't prove them."

"Wrong again. They can prove them easily. But most people aren't brave. They're ashamed to admit their mistakes. If it turns out, Mrs. Greenfield, that Zoe cheated you out of more than five thousand dollars and she spent it all—if she cheated you and you'll never see a penny of your money again—would you be willing to admit your mistake publicly? Would you be brave enough to prosecute her?"

"Those are such silly questions. Princess Zoe is a good woman. I believe in her. She is my best friend. Because of her, my son is alive."

The phone rang. Lanihan listened for a while, then hung up.

"Zoe's gone, Mrs. Greenfield. Cleared out. Gone with the wind. She took everything, even the wall sockets and the lighting fixtures."

"She'll be back," Momma said, with quiet confidence.

"Not unless you have something else she can steal."

"She's my friend, and when the time is right she'll come back. She has my address. She knows where to get in touch with me any time. I'll be hearing from Zoe. I have faith."

Lanihan hesitated. "It's peculiar faith—"

—For an orthodox Jew.... She finished his sentence in her head. "Then I must be a peculiar woman."

"No," he said gently, "just a mother."

TWENTY-THREE

Sunday, July 29, 1951

Momma was awake at six.

She felt alert and energetic immediately, the way she'd awakened in the mornings of her youth before life had sapped her strength. She was up, washed, and in her house dress, poaching eggs and toasting challah by the time Sol finished his morning prayers.

He barely spoke to her. So it had been between them for a long time....

***

In the weeks that had passed since Ike and Fanny brought her back from Police Headquarters, Sol had locked his anger up in silence.

After he'd asked Ike, "How much did they steal from her?"

"I don't know," Ike said. "The police know. But it was plenty, and now the Gypsies are gone. Disappeared."

Ike was sad and Sol was mute and angry, but Momma was content.

Detective Lanihan had kept his word. He was a gentleman. She was pleased that her family didn't know the size of the sum she'd invested. Five thousand dollars was, indeed, a lot.

It was a measure of her faith in Zoe; those who had no faith were better off not knowing.

Sol hadn't said another word then, and he'd said very little since. All through the *shiva* week, Momma, impatiently, had to move around him on his box. She'd insisted on scraping the Macintosh apples label off the side of the crate—who ever heard of keeping a box with labels pasted on it in a living room? She thought he would explode with rage when she came over with the knife and bent over and scraped, but he shut his eyes and sat still.

The silence was all right with Momma.

When Ben came back there would be time enough to talk.

Sol would be sorry. Oh, how he would apologize.

Instead of saying thank you to her for interceding, instead of being grateful for all she was accomplishing, he worried about money.

All right for him.

Her day would come.

Ike, too, was in mourning for the money.

Were *they* in for a surprise!

And those detectives: Lanihan, who knew so much, and Vitale, and Peggy Reilly—she must have seen plenty in her day even though she looked so fresh and innocent—they all thought they were so smart with their photographs and their Gypsy tales. The surprise was for them too.

Through all the steamy days of summer, Momma had remained placid and strong in her faith that she would ultimately show them, all of them.

Until yesterday.

Yesterday morning, *Shabbos*, Sol carried up a letter and handed it to her. It was addressed to *her*. She knew in an instant who it was from because she didn't belong to any organizations and no one ever wrote to her.

Only one person could be writing to her.

Princess Zoe!

All day Saturday she carried that sealed letter with her.

Whatever she did, wherever she went, the letter went too. Joy and curiosity slowed up her movement, but she kept the letter intact; it was forbidden to tear paper on the Sabbath. When she sat down to read the weekly stack of newspapers, the letter rested in her lap.

No newspaper story interested her this night; she read a line or two then glanced up at the clock, picked up the letter and held it up to the window trying to see through the envelope, gazed at the tree and the overgrown backyard, and then went back to the newspapers caring not at all for what she read.

At last, footsteps on the stairs. Sol was returning from shul. It was past sundown. Now she could tear open the envelope! Now she could put on the light!

Into the bathroom she hurried with her letter, carefully locking the door before she even put on the light. Then she sat down on the edge of the tub at the end farthest away from the toilet.

Sitting still, with her eyes closed, she asked God's forgiveness for opening *this* letter in such a profane place.

The flap lifted easily, a good omen.

Holding the lined note paper at the edge of her lap so she could make out the uneven writing, she read:

Ben will come. The insurance money is evil. Only this holds him back. Meet me at Western Union near your house, twelve o'clock Sunday and we'll make plans to burn the evil money and wellcome him back.

Your dear best friend

A jagged pain just behind her forehead dazed

Momma, so she just sat there for a long time, eyes shut, holding the paper. When the pain had lessened, she forced her eyes open a little and read it and then read it again, and then she folded it and put it back in its envelope. Promptly taking it out, she reread it one more time, put it away and then took it out once more.

Insurance money?

No one collects insurance money for a living person.

Insurance is collected by the living for the *dead.*

Insurance money for Ben could not be evil. Nor was it hers.

It could not be hers because Ben was alive and coming home.

She was not entitled to touch that money, dirty or clean, because she had a living son.

For Zoe to suggest she collect it was dishonest.

Dishonest? It was a scam.

So, after all, after all, Zoe was a crook.

Then...

Oh Zoe, Zoe, you son of a bitch, Momma thought wildly and then she thought it over and over again, allowing herself the incredible freedom of obscenity. *You son of a bitch. You bastard. You greedy bastard, you thief, you crook, you son of a bitch!* Her mind was tempted to use the F— word too, but she couldn't bring herself to do it even now.

I'll fix you, she resolved. I'll fix you good. You won't go 'round stealing money from mothers any more. For my darling, for my Ben's sake, I'll surprise you. The crybaby, the fool, the wet dishrag will surprise you, yes she will. Monsters like you should be in cages.

How could she get to Broome Street quickly?

Was anyone there on a Saturday night?

She had to try. Someone would be there, a clerk, a policeman, someone.

Sneaking out of the bathroom, she grabbed her purse and tiptoed downstairs. A taxi approached. She considered it, but it would be a long ride over the bridge and therefore very expensive. She let the taxi pass. She wouldn't be able to ride in it comfortably anyway. Every change on the meter would startle her, every additional nickel upset her.

Instead, she headed for the Marcy Avenue elevated train.

The trains at that hour were cruelly slow. To compound the agony, she made a mistake and got on a train that carried her to City Hall, but finally, finally, she arrived at Broome Street.

How Detective Lanihan looked at her when she walked in on him during this quiet hour on Saturday night! He simply couldn't believe that she was there. By herself. Without help from Ike or Fanny. From anyone.

He had thought she was just another stupid woman, just another weakling, a sucker. But when she marched in there with Zoe's letter in her hand, and when she told him about the insurance and how she knew she wasn't entitled to it, he'd grabbed her hand and given it a sturdy shake, a handclasp of respect.

"You're right," he said. "Zoe's a thief and she's not entitled to that money. But, Mrs. Greenfield," He tried to put it gently. "Mrs. Greenfield, you *are* entitled to it. Your son is dead. Zoe realizes that he's dead, and she's using your love for him to make herself some money. She could never understand, never never believe the kind of honesty that brought you here tonight."

"No," Momma said. "Not dead."

"Yes."

"Not dead, I say."

"Yes, Mrs. Greenfield. I'm sorry. Dead."

Huddled in the chair by his desk, she sat quietly trying to work her way through the morass. After a bit, she raised her head to look directly at him. "Not dead," she said.

This time he didn't argue. "You're going to keep this appointment tomorrow?"

"What do you think?"

"May my colleagues help you keep the appointment?" he asked

"Of course."

Once again he offered her his hand.

***

And so today was the rendezvous day. Sunday at noon.

The shopkeepers on Roebling Street would witness a sight they'd never dreamed of.

Elegant Mr. Tudor-Stuart would shake in his Fruit of the Loom underwear.

If there was time, Momma resolved, she would iron her best white blouse. First, she would do the breakfast dishes and put them away; next, she would dust-mop the floors and wipe the furniture. After that, she would wash the kitchen and bathroom linoleums. When all of this was finished, she would iron her blouse. She would wear it with her gray cotton skirt which was already washed and pressed, and she would also polish her shoes.

It was a good thing that Sol was off in shul.

He might not like it for his wife to be involved with the police in such a dangerous game.

Momma set to work vigorously, pausing now and again to smile into the empty rooms.

TWENTY-FOUR

At twenty to twelve, Momma had finished her ironing, just a last touch to each sleeve and a run of the iron down the front two panels to freshen them up. Then she was done.

Because of lack of time, she had checked in her closet to see if she could use one of the already pressed blouses which hung in wilted layers on her three hangers.

No.

A good citizen couldn't appear for police work in shabby garments.

The defendant—no, she must be the plaintiff—whoever she was, she could not be a slob.

She paused before the tarnished mirror and surveyed the plaintiff, her open, honest face, her broad brow, her deep face lines and gray hair. She thought of Princess Zoe's painted face and bejeweled neck. She thought of those cruel sharp fingernails.

Surely anyone would know in a minute the difference between the innocent woman and the guilty one.

How could a simple honest religious woman be expected to cope with black magic?

She set the iron on the stove to cool and gathered up the old blankets that were her ironing pad. She would have to move quickly or she'd be late.

***

At twenty to twelve, Detectives Reilly and Vitale were standing in the separate doorways of two stores on Roebling Street. Vitale had chosen a haberdashery entrance, much to the chagrin of the balding proprietor who kept glaring out at him. Peggy Reilly stood outside in the bright sunshine before a candy store. She appeared to be scanning the covers of the movie magazines on the newsstand.

A short, heavy woman, carrying two laden black-cloth shopping bags, came down the street from Broadway. Vitale noticed her first as she crossed at the far corner. He checked the time. Eleven forty-five.

The fortuneteller was early and Mrs. Greenfield was nowhere in sight!

The woman advanced in his direction moving in a waddling, small-stepped gait. She was dark-skinned and dark-eyed, her skirt almost to the ground; her hair was bound under a large white kerchief and from each ear hung a golden loop.

Then she was three stores away from him—
then two. Now she was in front of the candy store. He
raised his hand in signal and moved out onto the
sidewalk. Detective Reilly was on the other side
blocking the woman's escape.

She looked at the two of them, one on each
side of her.

"*Nem*," she protested. "*Nem. Nit csinálnak? Ki
az utamboi eged jenek át.*"

"Come over here. We want to talk to you,"
Detective Reilly said, leading the suspect into the
doorway of the haberdashery.

The woman made protesting noises but her
language was one that neither detective recognized
at all. Loud wails and yells but the words weren't
Romany. Both detectives had worked with Gypsies
long enough to recognize that. This one was playing
some complicated game.

"What the devil are you doing with that
woman?"

It was the haberdasher holding the door to the
store open, keeping his body safely inside while he
poked his head out. "I'll call the police. Let her go."

Vitale flashed his badge. "She's a Gypsy
fortuneteller. A swindler. We've a warrant for her."

"*Nem. Eresszenek!*" the captured woman
shouted. "*Hadd menjek rendört hivo. Segitség—
segitség—*"

Once he saw the badge, the haberdasher bravely allowed his body to emerge from the store. "She's no Gypsy. She's a Hasidic woman from the old country. She's speaking Hungarian."

The detectives were startled.

"These women pass by here all the time," the haberdasher went on. "Their special butcher has his shop on the next block. Look, there go two more just like her."

They looked, and to their dismay there were two more women similarly dressed and shopping-bagged walking across the street. Detective Vitale looked at his watch. Eleven fifty-five. He scanned the street anxiously. No Mrs. Greenfield in sight.

"You're positive?" he asked the haberdasher.

"Would I interfere if I wasn't positive? Look at her. She looks to you like a swindler?"

The captured woman, plain and plump, without makeup, her hair completely concealed by a white headcloth, was utterly dejected, collapsing now on her two laden shopping bags.

"Let her go," urged the haberdasher. "You got the wrong woman."

Detective Reilly let go of the captive's arm. The woman, amazed by her sudden freedom, didn't wait for explanations. She fled down Roebling Street, her two black bags flapping at her sides like swollen wings.

"What a story she'll tell tonight," the haberdasher grinned, rubbing his hands. Adventures like this didn't happen outside his store every day. "Thanks for the help." Vitale said. "You better get back inside—quick."

The haberdasher found his manners very abrupt, but he didn't protest. He moved fast. No doubt the police had their reasons. As he closed his door, he heard the woman detective warn, "Here she comes."

Watching through the plate glass window, he was amazed to see the two-handkerchief lady—the one who had asked for a gift box—and he started forward once more to open his door and tell those two cockamamie detectives that she was no Gypsy either. Then he decided to wait a minute and see.

The day was unusually hot and dusty, Momma noticed as she hurried along. Bright and hot. An occasional small breeze blew through Williamsburg, a hardly perceptible breeze probably a leftover from Manhattan or the Bronx.

As she approached the Western Union office, she heard her heart drumming and she began to count slowly to herself to achieve calmness. She spotted Detective Reilly, in the same brown silk suit, reading magazine covers on the newsstand; she saw a man loitering in the haberdashery entrance. Yes, it was Vitale.

Momma did not in any way acknowledge that she knew them. She just came along and stopped in front of the telegraph store window.

The Catholic church's bells chimed the noon hour.

Momma resented this invasion of her privacy. Christmas time the bells played carols. What could Jews do about it? It was a shame that they were forced to listen to Christian music.

Across the street, the splendid black convertible drew up. Princess Zoe got out at once and came hurrying across the street to greet her friend. Momma stepped forward fearlessly as the fortuneteller neared the curb, but in front of Momma suddenly were the detectives. First, Detective Vitale with his gun drawn—and then Peggy Reilly, looking grim.

She too had a gun.

Zoe stopped and stood rigid. From the car, her husband came running, bigger and swarthier than Momma remembered him. Momma's knees were trembling, and she lost control of herself slightly and was grateful for her two pair of thick underpants.

"What's all this?" the husband demanded.

"Keep quiet," Zoe snapped. "Call my father."

"Not now," Vitale said. "First we'll go over to the station house. We have warrants for both of you."

Detective Reilly brought handcuffs out of her purse for Princess Zoe, who glared at Momma but said nothing. Vitale handcuffed the husband's wrist to his own then said, "We're going in here for a minute," indicating the haberdashery.

"Would you give the lady out there a chair—and a drink of water?" Vitale asked the haberdasher, who by then was almost prostrate with excitement.

"Certainly. She's a customer of mine. Just a few weeks ago I sold her some men's handkerchiefs." He scurried into his back room and brought forth a folding chair.

Momma sat gratefully, oblivious of the gathering crowd. Her earlier elation was gone. She was exhausted. The haberdasher brought her a glass of water and she emptied it at once.

"How did your husband like those handkerchiefs you bought from me?" he asked loudly, establishing his relationship with her publicly.

She didn't answer.

The others came out of the store.

"Come along, Mrs. Greenfield," Detective Vitale said. "You were very brave. I'll tell Lanihan. You're a strong woman to keep going after all you've been through."

Momma tried to smile at him, to acknowledge his kindness. "Thank you," she said.

Princess Zoe spat on the sidewalk.

***

"We're booking them now," Peggy Reilly told Momma as she sat in the cool dark anteroom of the station house. "Soon it will be all over for you and you must start trying to forget it. As if it were a very bad dream."

"No, I will not forget, not for one minute." Momma's eyes were wet but she did not cry. "A missing son is not an easy thing for a mother—"

Reproachfully, she looked across at Princess Zoe who was standing before the railing, her big husband at her side, as Vitale gave the police clerk information.

"How could you do such a thing, Zoe, to your friend?" Momma asked. "How could you? I'm sure it was all your husband's idea, but how could you try to cheat me with my son missing? If you needed money, you could have asked. I would have been glad to do what I could for you. After all you did for me."

Zoe looked back over her shoulder. "You wanted to give your money away. If not me, someone else would have got it."

Her husband muttered something to her, but she tossed her head defiantly and then turned back to Momma. "He's not missing," she said. "He's dead!"

Momma screwed up her eyes as if dazzled by a sudden, glaring, too-bright light. A great blazing bird seemed to have invaded her head, and its wings beat flutteringly upon her brain.

"A lot you know." She could barely whisper it. "I would like to go home now, Peggy," she said. "Please—I would like to go to my home."

TWENTY-FIVE

Sol sat alone in the shul.

He knew the *shammes* was waiting outside to lock up, still he sat looking up at the rows and rows of empty red plush seats like open mouths howling at him.

"God," he pleaded silently, "no more wars. No more wars, God, I beg of you. I have no more sons to die, but other people have sons. God, for them, stop the wars." He tipped his head back so he was looking straight up. All he saw was the blue domed ceiling and the white stars stippled there.

"God, You gave me my child so late in life that it was a miracle, and then You took him away from me. I wouldn't ask why, God. It's not my place. But it was a terrible thing to do to me and Momma. We tried. All our lives we tried the best we knew to please You. And we had hard lives, the hardest; but we never forgot You. Still, You punished us.

"How is it that a Stein lives and flourishes with real estate and cars, and he has children and grandchildren, and a Sol Greenfield crawls all his life like a thirsty man in the desert seeking one small drink of happiness. And when he gets the drink, it's poisoned. How is it, God, that You let war finish a lovely thing that You started? Forgive me for envying Stein, God. I am ashamed. Don't think I'm not ashamed. But I do envy his living children and his grandchildren, in my shame.

"And my Ben. He could not have displeased You, for he was young and innocent, and his sins were too small to anger You in Your greatness. Yet You cut him down in Your infinite wisdom which I do not question. I would only like a little to understand how it is, God, that war must come to destroy the most beautiful and innocent and very young of the world. How is it that the corrupt politicians, the moneymakers and the haters go on and on?

"I am willing, God, I *must* believe in You, but You have taken my boy and returned him to the dust and I am trying to understand. I promise, God, that I will never doubt You. I will obey as I always have. I will pray and observe and be as good a Jew as I can until my last breath, but I must tell you, God, I cannot understand.

"From men I get many words for answers when I ask these questions, God. Many words. From the government comes printed words, and from friends, spoken words and written messages on cards in fruit baskets. But words are nothing for they are easily spoken and easily forgotten.

"The reason, God. I am asking the reason, for in Your great wisdom and mercy there must surely be a reason why I, Solomon Greenfield, a presser, an unsuccessful man, and my wife Eva, a devoted mother and housewife, why we had to lose our child in a far-off country which is no better off for his death. A country we never even heard of till the last couple of years. Only let me understand a little, God, only that and I will be silent.

"Please, God. Please help me."

"Greenfield," the *shammes* said from behind him, "I must lock up now."

Sol stumbled to his feet. "Sure. Lock up now. I'm sorry if I kept you. I thought I would get a little comfort if I sat here awhile, a little understanding maybe. But for me there is no comfort left on this earth."

"Take." The *shammes* offered his snuffbox. "It will clear your head."

"That would be magic," Sol said sadly. "I don't believe in magic."

TWENTY-SIX

Wearily he climbed the stairs in the dark hall. He heard Momma's voice but he couldn't make out what she was saying or who she was talking to.

He turned the knob.

The room was gray, its shabbiness softened by the half-light of dusk. Momma was sitting on an apple crate near the window where she could see Nature. She was weeping.

She was in stockinged feet.

She was wearing her best white blouse and a neat gray skirt. The blouse had a long cut down the front as if a knife had slashed it.

She looked up at him but she continued to speak softly, to go on with what she was doing.

She was saying Yiskor, the prayer of remembrance. *"Mayest Thou, O God, remember the soul of my dear son who has gone to his eternal home. O may his soul be bound up in the bond of life, and may he be at peace, with fullness of joy in Thy presence for evermore. Amen."*

He came further into the room to stand beside her, and together they mourned.

Sheila Solomon Klass has been teaching English since 1965 at Manhattan Community College of The City University of New York where she holds a full professorship. She did her undergraduate work at Brooklyn College and received her MA and MFA degrees from the Writers' Workshop at the State University of Iowa.

She has worked as an aide in a psychiatric hospital and as a teacher in a junior high school. She has been a United States Information Service lecturer in Creative Writing at several women's colleges in Calcutta, India and has held lectureships at the University of Connecticut and at the Leonia Library, Leonia, New Jersey.

She has received a First Prize in Fiction Award from the Charles Goldman Judaica Library and a Citation as a Notable New Jersey Author from the New Jersey Institute of Technology. Her research materials and early drafts of *In a Cold Open Field* were exhibited in a month-long show at the Leonia Library.

She has published more than fifty articles, short stories, and reviews in a variety of magazines and journals, including *The New York Times Book Review, The New York Times,* and *Working Mother.* She has published four novels as well as ten novels for young adults and a memoir.

Ms. Klass is listed in *Contemporary Authors, Who's Who of American Women, Who's Who in the East,* and *The International Authors and Writers Who's Who.*